# BATTER UP

## By JACKSON SCHOLZ

Batter Up

Fielder from Nowhere

JACKSON SCHOLZ

# BATTER UP

*Morrow Junior Books* • NEW YORK

Library of Congress Cataloging-in-Publication Data
Scholz, Jackson. Batter up  /  Jackson Scholz.  p.  cm.
Summary: Marty Shane, a powerful hitter and part owner of a major
league baseball club, is determined to use his talents, not his
connections, to play for a professional team.
ISBN 0-688-12485-2
[1. Baseball—Fiction.]  I. Title.  PZ7.S37Bat  1993
[Fic]—dc20  92-32796  CIP  AC

# BATTER UP

# CHAPTER 1

_____

_____

There was reason for Marty Shane to believe that the approaching conference would be fraternal in name only, that the true spirit of brotherly love and understanding would be absent in a big way.

Marty's belief was not without foundation. It was based upon the evidence of past events, namely, that he and his older brother, Bender Shane, had never clicked and probably never would.

Marty held no one responsible for this. It was one of those things—brought on and fostered by a pair of divergent natures which stemmed from the same root but perversely grew in opposite directions.

Bender Shane was a chip off the old block, a counterpart of their father, Corkey Shane, to whom baseball had been the breath of life. It had been said affectionately of Corkey Shane that his hide had been of a quality to cover baseballs, but, true or false, he had made the grade and had left as an inheritance to his sons controlling interest in the big league Quakers.

Bender, like his father, was solid, tough, and practical. He had made full use of all these qualities in his upward battle through the big league ranks. He was managing the Quakers now, and managing them well.

With due respect to his ripe old age of thirty-four, he was easing himself gradually out of active competition. He could still patrol the keystone area with speed and skill when necessity demanded or when he felt the urge to play, but for the most part he seemed content to let the younger men take over. It was a matter of shrewd business.

"When I begin to slip," he said, "I'm going to quit. But when I finally have to pack my uniform in mothballs, I want to know I've trained some first-rate men to fill my spot at second base."

Marty Shane, twelve years his brother's junior, had been cut from a different pattern. He possessed the flash and glitter that his brother lacked. He thought faster, moved more swiftly. A driving restlessness was evident in all his motions, a constant flexibility of mind and muscles.

Both parents had been dead some years, yet the interval had caused no tightening of fraternal bonds. The reverse, probably, had happened and partly because of circumstances. Marty had gone to college. Bender had merely finished high school. Marty had seen action in the Pacific in World War II. He had earned a Silver Star and had been honorably discharged. Bender had fumed and griped at home because a former beanball accident had kept him out of the service.

Marty Shane was heading toward his brother's office now. Bender had asked him to show up there, a fact which was significant. It meant a business conference, and Marty frankly had no liking for business conferences—this conference in particular, because he had a strong hunch as to the trend it undoubtedly would take. Bender, through a dogged sense of duty, probably believed it necessary to discuss Marty's future, and would probably assume the older brother role of stern adviser. Bender was like that.

Marty's suspicions were almost immediately confirmed when he entered the Quakers' clubhouse through the street door and went back to Bender's

3

office. Bender was sitting behind his desk. He looked up and said with blunt gruffness:

"Hi, Marty. It's time we had a powwow. Grab a chair."

Marty said, "Okay," and started across the office toward a chair beside his brother's desk. He was not resentful of his brother's tone because he sensed in it an effort to be casual, an effort to mask the embarrassment both men felt.

It was more evident in Bender than in Marty. Marty possessed more worldliness and poise—or at least he believed he did. He accepted the fact that he and his brother were virtual strangers despite their common parentage. That's the way it was. Why try to change it? With the possible exception of baseball they had no mutual interests, no mutual characteristics. Why, therefore, reasoned Marty, should either of them try to bridge the gap merely because they happened to be brothers?

Some stubborn quirk in Bender Shane prevented him from looking at the thing that way. He had a bulldog streak which insisted situations should be worked out by the book—even brotherhood. Recognizing this in Bender, Marty was quietly amused. He sat down and waited for Bender to push his thoughts in line.

4

There was no physical resemblance between the men. Bender was blocky, dark-haired, square-faced. Marty Shane was tall, almost six feet, with long smooth muscles laid along his frame. At first glance he appeared slender; a second glance disproved it. He had a width of shoulder and a depth of chest that spoke of power. He had a way of moving which came close to being cocky.

His eyes confirmed it. They were gray, wide-set, but they looked upon the world with too much boldness. They lacked the caution and the compromise of sound maturity. There was a restless discontent behind their steadiness, an expression many men had brought back from the battle front.

His features lacked the rugged contour of his brother's. His face was longer, and the bones stood out more sharply. His lips were mobile, quick to laugh, and quick to harden when his temper hit him. He was a man geared high, stretched taut, but nicely balanced in a way most people seemed to like. He made friends easily, and held them, because Marty Shane liked almost everybody. His brother finally said:

"It's this way, Marty. You ought to go back to school."

"What for?"

The question annoyed Bender, but he had obviously expected something of the sort and had steeled himself to patience. He said with marked restraint:

"You got too much on the ball, Marty, and it's a shame to waste it. School has always been easy for you. You got into college when you were sixteen. You enlisted in the Air Force as soon as you were old enough, but you had time to finish three years of college before they called you. You ought to go back and get your sheepskin."

"I suppose so," agreed Marty indifferently. "But I can't whip up the interest. College would be pretty dull after what I've been through."

"Then look at it this way. You started something. Why not finish it? It's a good habit to get into."

"Sure," conceded Marty with a shrug.

Bender's patience began to wear a little thin. "If you won't go back to school," he said, "then you ought to get a job. You're spending too much of your daytime in the hay and too much of your night-time in nightclubs."

"It's my business."

"Yeah, sure. You're a returned soldier. You need a period of adjustment. You've got to have time to find yourself. I know all those answers, Marty, but after all you've had six months to settle down."

Marty hunched himself resignedly in his chair.

6

His pantomime was good. It said, Let's get the lecture over with.

Bender said, "Okay, I'm being hammy. I know I'm wastin' wind, but I've got a one-track mind, so I've got to get it off my chest."

"I'm listening."

"From the looks of things," said Bender grimly, "you can keep on loafing for a long time if you want to. You've got a twenty-five percent chunk of the Quakers, and the club's making money. All you have to do is to coast along and enjoy yourself. If that's the way you want it, we'll let it ride. I just thought maybe you'd like to get your feet on the ground again, and I figured I'd like to help you do it."

Marty sobered, feeling somewhat like a heel. Bender meant well. He was a right guy, even though Marty still believed him to be dull company. Marty said, "Thanks, Bender. There's a lot to what you say. I've even been giving the matter a little thought myself—as little as possible. I've just about decided, though, to take up baseball."

"*What*?" It was a cry of honest protest, carrying the suggestion of mild outrage. In Marty's opinion it verged closely upon insult. His ire was stirred.

"What's wrong with baseball?" he demanded sharply.

Pulling himself together, Bender tried diplomacy which, at best, was clumsy. He said, "Look, Marty. You can get a college education. You shouldn't waste it. You've got brains enough to be a big shot if you'd settle down."

Marty eyed his brother steadily. Then he said, "Don't try to kid me, guy. You don't think I *could* make the grade in baseball."

Bender hauled in a deep breath, then shrugged resignedly.

"Frankly, Marty, I don't. Not in big league baseball."

"I batted .420 in my junior year at college."

"Yeah, I know," admitted Bender. "You also tried to play first base."

"*Tried*?"

"This time don't try to kid *me*," Bender told him pointedly. "I've forgotten more baseball than you'll ever know. You've got more natural ability, Marty, than either Dad or I ever had. That's your trouble. It's never occurred to you, and probably never will, that learning to play top-flight baseball is a long hard job. Frankly, Marty, I don't think you've got the patience or the stamina to tackle a job of that sort. I'd hate to see you try."

"In other words, you're trying to say I'd be a disgrace to the family if I never got beyond the minors."

8

"Maybe that's what I mean," admitted Bender.

They were definitely glaring at each other now. The tempers of both men were getting frayed. It was the sort of showdown Marty had not anticipated, and he felt a strange reluctance to let the thing get out of hand. He didn't want an open break. Bender must have felt the same way. Picking up a pencil from his desk he stared at it awhile, then said, "Look, kid. Let's talk this over sensibly."

"Okay," said Marty. In a sense he was relieved, but underneath this feeling ran conviction that he'd crossed a borderline he could not recross.

He had made a decision, or maybe he had been forced into one. It didn't matter. The momentous part was the decision itself, the first important one he'd made since his discharge from the Air Force. He was going to play baseball. Probably he should have known it all the time, should have recognized the fact that baseball was a part of him. He was conscious of a feeling of excitement.

Bender, his voice controlled, said, "Where do you intend to play?"

"I'll find a spot."

Bender studied his pencil carefully and said, "I could farm you out."

"No dice," said Marty promptly. "I'll call my own shots."

Bender let his breath out slowly. It sounded like

9

a relieved sigh, an indication he didn't want to be responsible for Marty.

"Any ideas?" Bender asked.

Marty had none but didn't want to admit it, so he pulled one from a hat. "The Bantams in Buffalo have a snappy club with no big league hookup. I think I'll take a shot at that."

Bender's big head came up with a jerk. "Lay off the Bantams!" he ordered bluntly.

It was not the proper way to handle Marty Shane. His chin pushed forward slightly.

"Why?" he asked.

Bender's mouth started to open in reply, then slowly closed. He scowled a moment, then said, "To start with, I've advised you against taking up baseball. It was wasted effort. Now I advise you against the Bantams. It's probably wasted effort too."

"That's right," admitted Marty.

"It's your funeral, kid," said Bender tightly.

"Send me lilies," Marty said, getting to his feet.

Bender made a restraining motion with his hand. "There's another matter, Marty," he said, "a strictly business matter. You own twenty-five percent of the Quakers' stock. I own thirty percent, which gives us controlling interest."

"Yeah, I know," said Marty impatiently. "And the other forty-five percent is owned by the daughter of Dad's old partner, an old maid by the name of Alma Parker."

"How'd you know she was an old maid?" asked Bender curiously.

"I saw the legal papers. She's a spinster."

"Uh-huh," Bender said. "But that's beside the point. The point is, I've been running this club and making it pay. I need controlling interest to be sure I can keep it up. That means your stock and my stock, so it would make things a lot simpler if you'd give me your power of attorney."

Marty stiffened. "Meaning I might sell my shares and cross you up?"

"No, confound it! I don't mean it that way. I don't think you'd cross me up deliberately, but you've been throwing so much dough around lately that you might find yourself hard up. If you'd use your head you'd see that I'm merely trying to protect your interests, and assure your source of income."

A perverse stubbornness took hold of Marty. He said, "I like the setup as it is. I'll handle my own stock." He headed toward the door.

"Then nuts to you!" roared Bender.

"And nuts to you, dear brother," answered Marty from the doorway.

# CHAPTER 2

_____

_____

Marty Shane did not see Bender Shane for some time after that. Three days later Bender took his Quakers to their training camp in Florida. Through inquiries, Marty learned that the Buffalo Bantams were training down in Pine Mound, South Carolina, but he restrained himself from going there at once.

Instead, he went back to his alma mater, Dartmouth, where he was received with great enthusiasm, particularly by the baseball coach and members of the team. The enthusiasm dwindled slightly when they found out he had not returned for the purpose of finishing his college education, but they were glad to see him just the same, and glad to include him in the baseball workouts.

The indoor training quarters, it is true, were cramped, but the huge batting net was up, a matter which concerned Marty more than any other feature. Batting was his dish. He spent considerable time inside the net while the college pitchers served them up to him.

His batting eye was not as rusty as he'd feared. Flying a Mustang in air combat against Japanese Zeros had obviously kept his eyesight keen and his reactions swift. His timing at the plate was a little off at first, but it improved with satisfying speed. In a few days he was belting the apple on the nose consistently, and when a week of concentrated work had passed, he knew his old skill was intact.

It was time now for him to pack his bag and head for the Bantam training camp, but something held him back—a reluctance to leave, which annoyed him a trifle. He had returned for this brief visit with a set idea that he had matured beyond the age of college men and their activities, but was finding now it wasn't so. He liked it, found it easy to let the familiar college atmosphere surround him.

He delayed his trip south for another week, telling himself he needed further tuning up. Well, maybe he did. But he stretched things a bit by convincing himself he'd better tune up on his boxing too. He'd been a pretty good fighter during his last year at school, and he liked the sport. So he spent part of his spare hours in the boxing room, swapping leather with the students.

The pleasant interlude, however, could not last forever, and the day approached when he finally had to tear himself away. It required an effort which surprised him, made him wonder if he hadn't made a big mistake in the conference with his brother. It wasn't too late, of course, to change his mind. He considered the idea, then rejected it. He'd made his boast that he could make the grade in big league baseball, and he'd have to see it through. He was built that way.

So he finally packed his grip and headed south. He didn't enjoy the train trip much. He was gloomy and somewhat apprehensive, wondering with recurring spasms of clammy doubt if he hadn't stuck out his neck about a mile too far.

He had not advised the Bantams' manager, Lobo Mercer, of his intention to play first base for the Bantams. This was a matter, Marty reasoned, which might be discussed with more success after he had battered a few horsehides out of shape. It was the most convincing argument he could think of, and he was reasonably certain that the manager of any B team like the Bantams would give him all the chances he needed to advance the argument.

Marty left the train at a jerkwater station with the name of Pine Mound painted in weathered letters upon the station building. It was worse than he had feared. The town was a lethargic sprawling place of moderate size, surrounded by pine trees and sand. Marty regarded the visible portion of the town with frank dismay. He eased his suitcase to the warped boards of the platform, took off his hat, pulled out a handkerchief and mopped the perspiration from his forehead. He was running the handkerchief around the inside of his hat when a voice beside him said, " 'Scuse me, sir. Are you a Bantam man?"

Marty turned, looked down, and met the white-toothed grin of a youngster in his early teens. Marty grinned too, and said, "Well, no. But I'm looking for a Bantam man—the boss."

"That's Mr. Mercer."

Marty nodded. "Can you tell me where to find him?"

"Yes, *sir*. He's out playin' with the boys. Battin' that ol' horsehide."

"How do I get there?"

" 'Tain't but a short piece. I can lead you."

"You've earned two-bits. Lead on, Macduff."

"Name's William," corrected Marty's new guide. "This way, sir."

A walk of ten minutes brought them to the Bantams' training field, and Marty Shane was not impressed by what he saw. Far from it. Up to this point he believed he had made full allowance for the difference in financial status between a minor league club and a big league club, but even his most generous allowance had failed to prepare him for the dusty lumpy diamond upon which the men were training.

"So *this* is it," he said.

"Yes, *sir*," said William proudly.

Marty paid the quarter he had promised, then asked, "Which one is Mr. Mercer?"

"That big one battin' fungos," William said with awe.

"Okay—and thank you, William."

"Thank *you*, sir," William said.

Marty started toward the "big one battin' fungos." He was big all right, with the heavy-middled bigness that would never again permit him to field grounders or run bases. He looked like what he was—a big leaguer gone to seed.

His head was massive, and his neck was thick. Perspiration was pouring from him, despite which he was wearing a heavy sweatshirt in an obvious effort to melt away a portion of his excess suet. His features were heavy but not dumb. When he turned toward him, Marty felt the impact of the big man's

16

eyes, whose paleness made them look unnaturally cold and calculating. They were shrewd, fast-thinking eyes.

They tackled a job, though, when they rested upon Marty Shane. Familiar as Lobo Mercer was with kids who bummed their way for miles to try out with the Bantams, he was having trouble cataloging Marty. Mercer probably pegged him as a baseball player, but knew right well that baseball players wearing hundred-dollar tailored suits did not show up, just unannounced, at class B training camps. Not looking for a job, at any rate.

"Something I can do for you?" asked Mercer cautiously.

"Why, yes. I'd like to try out with the Bantams."

Mercer, though still slightly puzzled, was finding himself on more familiar ground. He said, "We're pretty well filled up."

"You've nothing to lose by giving me a chance to show what I can do," said Marty mildly.

"Where've you played?"

"Dartmouth."

"Position?"

"First."

"Batting average?"

"Four-twenty my last year."

Mercer showed a guarded interest. "What's your name?"

"Shane. Marty Shane."

Something happened to Mercer's eyes. An opaque curtain dropped in front of them. The muscles of his face went stiff and hard.

"I haven't got a spot for you," he said and turned away.

It required several seconds for Marty to recover from his first surprise. Then a slow stubborn anger crept upon him. His lips lost their mobility as they tightened at the corners. The color of his eyes appeared to change from warm gray to the darker shade of storm clouds. He wasn't geared to crude brush-offs like this.

He said, "Hold on a minute, Mercer. You're cutting your own throat."

Turning back, the big man said, "It's my throat, Shane."

"You need a slugger in your club—a cleanup man."

Mercer's eyelids flickered, involuntary acknowledgment that Marty Shane had scored a bull's-eye.

"Who told you that?"

"I found it out before I came here."

"Okay, I need a slugger. But you're not it, kid. Beat it."

Marty was sore by this time, a condition which worked against his common sense and sabotaged his caution.

18

"I can knock any bush league pitcher *you've* got off the mound," he snapped.

Lobo Mercer thought this over in a way that made Marty wish he'd kept his mouth shut. However, it was too late to back out now. There was obvious amusement in Mercer's eyes as he rubbed the stubble on his chin. He needled, "So you're *that* good, huh?"

"You know how to find out," said Marty, backing his play doggedly.

Mercer nodded slowly. "Well, Shane, you may be right. You wouldn't care to prove it right now, would you?"

"Now or any time," growled Marty.

"Okay, kid, you asked for it," said Mercer. "And I'm sort of glad you did. My boys're getting a little bored. They need some fun." He raised his voice and bellowed, "Come in here, gang!"

The Bantams, smelling entertainment, came jogging in. They formed a grinning circle around Marty and Mercer. Mercer told them solemnly: "We have a young man here named Shane. He admits he's good. He went to college and he slaughtered all the pitchers in his league. The hurlers who faced him were led sobbing from the mound. With blushing modesty he claims he can slaughter all the pitchers in *our* league, and that we have to see. He's been kind enough to offer us a demonstra-

19

tion—free." Mercer turned to a big man in the group and asked, "How about it, Mugger? Would you like to toss the lad a few?"

A sharp bell of warning rang in Marty's brain. Included in the incidental information he had picked up on the Bantams was the fact that Mugger Blain was on their roster. It was an item which had slipped his mind during the turmoil of his anger, but now it loomed importantly. There was trouble ahead, and plenty of it.

# CHAPTER 3

Mugger Blain was fresh from the big time. He had not been shunted to the minors because his arm had failed, but because he couldn't get along with umpires and because he couldn't keep away from nightclubs. He had promised to reform, and was trying to stage his comeback on the Bantam club.

Blain stepped forward, a pleased grin on his horselike face. Playing up to Mercer, Blain said, "Well, now, Lobo, I've always been sort of scared of these college hot shots, but if you say so I'll take a chance on gettin' my hat knocked off."

"Let's go then," Mercer said. "And just to make it legal, we'll have fielders." He rattled off a list of names to fill the positions. Then turning to Marty he asked, "Want some shoes?"

"I've got my own," said Marty. He opened his suitcase, took out his cleats, and careless of his expensive suit sat down in the dirt to change. He took out his baseball cap to shade his eyes, then shed his coat.

Twinges of apprehension began to sneak along his nerves as he went to the bat pile and selected a bat whose balance suited him. It began to dawn on him he'd stuck his neck out so far he felt like a giraffe. If Mugger Blain was in any sort of shape, he'd be plain poison to a guy who'd never faced any but college pitchers.

While Marty swung a pair of bats to stretch his arms, he saw Mercer pulling on the catcher's tools. Mercer had been a backstop in his prime. He now announced, "I'm actin' as ump, too, Shane. I'll call 'em as I see 'em."

Marty could have wished for a better setup, but realized he was in no position to demand one. Nevertheless, he saw a faint glimmer of hope as he watched Blain, a big right-hander, throw some warm-up balls.

Blain, as yet, had not worked off his winter fat. There was a droop about his middle and a looseness to his face which suggested he had not forgone his night life—yet. There was a punch to his delivery, but no fur on it. There wasn't enough speed there to worry Marty. He liked them fast. The thing that worried him was that Blain might bend his hooks in exactly where he wanted them.

"Ready, Mugger?" Mercer called.

"Yeah, lemme have 'im," Blain said greedily.

Mercer pulled on his cage and said through the bars, "Okay, Shane. Come and get it."

Marty stepped into the right-hand batter's box, his bat upon his shoulder. None of his cockiness was with him now. He was tense, too tense, realizing he had talked himself into a jam.

Blain gave him a long deliberate size-up, relishing the moment. He made considerable business of receiving Mercer's signal, mulling it over in his mind, then nodding his approval. By the time Blain finally put his foot against the slab, Marty Shane was jumpy as a flea.

The truth, with all its alarming force, had finally smacked him. For the first time in his life he was face to face with a big league pitcher, with more at stake than he cared to think about.

He tried to shake his muscles loose as Blain started his compact windup. He must have shaken a few of his muscles loose, at any rate, because Blain's first delivery didn't tear his elbows off as it

23

otherwise might have done. It was a letter-skimmer, and Marty managed to get his elbows up in time.

The worst part, however, was the uncontrollable reflex of Marty's legs. They drove him back as if he'd just discovered a rattlesnake coiled upon the plate. It puzzled him, because he wasn't skittish of close balls. It was immediate proof of the bad condition of his nerves, a proof which had a prompt and salutary effect on him. It made him mad, a condition improved by the yapping comment of the shortstop: "Watch 'im, Lobo! Catch 'im when he faints!"

Marty's lips thinned out once more as he snugged his spikes into the dirt. This was something he could understand. Mugger Blain had tried to dust him off. It was the old nanny-getting business from which Marty grabbed a quick significance. Maybe Blain wasn't as hot as he was supposed to be. Maybe he had to soften up a batter first. The explanation suited Marty, at any rate.

Mercer yelled, "Ball one!" and lobbed the ball back to Blain.

Marty settled himself again, relaxed this time. His brain was working too. He matched it against Blain's and Mercer's. He counted on another duster—and it came. This time Marty put on a show.

He jumped back like a kangaroo, pretending panic. The Bantams smothered him with razzberries.

"Ball two!" yelled Mercer.

Marty stepped back to the plate. He did it with a shamefaced nervous haste, as if he had to get in there before his courage failed him. He feared he might be spreading it on a little thick, but the Bantams were having too much fun to be suspicious.

The next pitch was a natural. It had to be a hook. Shane obviously had been softened up for one. It was the artistic thing to throw, a hook aimed at the batter but bending in across the plate. A pitch like that would be almost certain to cause a rattled batter to jump away from a clean strike.

Marty wiggled his cleats into the dirt while Mugger Blain took enough time on the mound to build a chicken coop. When he finally made his heave, it looked like another close one, but Marty, trusting his judgment, watched it like a hawk. When it began to bend, he swung—a short slash with power behind his wrists.

He could tell by the solid impact that he'd really tagged that one. The witty shortstop might have knocked it down if he'd been on his toes, but, concentrating as he was on his next wisecrack, the ball went past him like a bolt of lightning. He turned and stared at it. The other Bantams also stared.

Mugger Blain was still half crouched in the position of finishing his pitch. His head twisted grotesquely across his shoulder as his eyes followed the direction of the ball.

Gradually all eyes, including Blain's, came back to Marty Shane, who withstood the scrutiny deadpan. He was not taking time out to congratulate himself. He was keeping his mind riveted on the job ahead, for he knew that Mugger Blain would settle down to business now. Marty expected some comment from Lobo Mercer, but Mercer addressed his words to Blain. He said, "The college boy outguessed you, Mugger."

"Outguessed *me*?" Blain bellowed. "Who gave the signs?"

"Okay," conceded Mercer. "He outguessed *us*. We'll chalk up one for him. Let's go."

Blain tried another close one, but the feel of that clean bingle had wiped out Marty's jitters. When the pitch came in he raised his elbows, hauled in his stomach, and let the fireball sizzle past his shirt.

"Ball one," decided Mercer.

Blain got the ball back, polished it in his mitt, and glared at Marty. Marty reached for his cap in a casual gesture to pull the visor lower. In the process he permitted his thumb to rest for an instant on his nose, then wiggled his fingers briefly as he released the brim. It was a fleeting gesture, but

Blain didn't miss it. His face went red and he made an involuntary motion to leave the mound. He checked himself in time and toed the slab. He whipped the ball in fast without a windup, and Marty really *watched* that one.

It was well he did. It was a good old-fashioned beanball with no frills on it. Marty hit the dirt with time to spare. He came up grinning. He said to Mercer, "Playful, isn't he?"

But Mercer acted as if he hadn't heard. Taking a few quick steps toward Blain he rasped, "Did I call for *that* one, Mugger?"

"No," Blain admitted sullenly. "But you didn't see what that young punk pulled on me."

"I saw it," Mercer told him shortly. "And any man in the league is liable to pull the same thing on you. If you can't take it, Mugger, you're not good enough for me. I want a pitcher, not a sorehead. Now let's see you pitch."

"Okay," said Blain sourly. "But watch them soft old mitts of yours. I'll burn 'em off."

"I hope you do," snapped Mercer. "It'll prove you're good."

Blain threw a curve ball next. He had stuff on it, but Marty nicked it for a foul outside the first base line. The fourth delivery was a change of pace, a neat one. It almost fooled Marty, but he got a chunk of that one too, a foul behind third base.

With a two–two count they tried Marty with a fast one just above the knees. Marty didn't like it. It was too far out. He let it go, then wished he'd gone for it. It was a close decision any way you looked at it, and he was certain Mercer would call it for a strike-out. He was surprised when Mercer said, "Ball three." Marty's respect for him went up a notch.

Blain didn't like the call, but he kept his mouth shut. He took Mercer's signal for the payoff ball. Marty gambled on a drop hook, and guessed right. In fact he almost outguessed himself by overestimating Blain's ability. Marty swung too low, barely clipping the underside of the ball. The foul zinged back over Mercer's head.

With the count still full, Blain sent in another hook. It was a good one, but not spectacular. This time Marty made allowances for its limitations, swung hard, and bopped it on the nose. It went screeching over second base for a clean hit to center field.

There was no comment from the Bantams, but their mental attitudes had changed. It was apparent in their postures. The infielders instead of standing indifferently erect were half bent now, their hands upon their knees.

Marty sensed the new tension all around him but tried not to let it creep into his own bones. He didn't kid himself. He wasn't out of the woods yet. There was still the big chance that Blain might settle down and make a chump of him.

Blain tried with everything he had, but the thing Marty had suspected was soon verified. Blain wasn't in shape yet. His control was not yet grooved, nor were his hooks as wicked as they should have been. In his present state he was no more formidable than a first-rate college hurler.

Marty demonstrated this in a businesslike, cold-blooded manner. He kept his eye on the ball and plastered it all over the field. His wallops weren't all hits, but they gave the Bantams some snappy fielding practice.

They seemed to be enjoying it, and their attitude puzzled Marty until it finally dawned on him the Bantams were enjoying the shellacking he was handing Mugger Blain. Obviously Blain wasn't very popular.

He got no better fast. Marty murdered his best deliveries. The payoff came when Marty uncorked his Sunday punch against a careless fast one dead across the center of the plate. The ball sailed far above the left fielder's head—a round-trip ticket in any league. Marty Shane was hot today.

At this point Lobo Mercer called things off. He had been silent for some time, and when he finally said, "Okay, I've seen enough," Marty went on the defensive, quickly formulating a few apt remarks to counter any face-saving devices Lobo Mercer might employ.

Marty needn't have bothered, though, because Mercer didn't try to save face. He was grinning when he pulled his mask off, a grin of admission that he'd made a losing guess. He said, "Pick up the marbles, Marty. I missed the boat. You can belt 'em kid, and I apologize for doubting it."

The sudden reversal of Mercer's attitude puzzled Marty. There was something going on in Mercer's brain which Marty couldn't fathom. The feeling was insistent, strong, yet he had nothing with which to back it up. It was hard to doubt the sincerity of Mercer's present attitude, and when a guy apologized as honestly as that—well, it wasn't a characteristic of Marty's friendly nature to rub it in. He said, "Shucks, that's all right. I guess I shot my mouth off pretty loud."

"Can you field as well as you can hit?" asked Mercer.

"Well, no," admitted Marty frankly. "I guess I can't. It seems like—well, I'm mostly interested in batting. I *like* to bat."

"And you don't like to field?"

"Well, yes, I like that too, but I don't get quite as much kick out of it."

Mercer thought this over with a carefulness that

made Marty wish he hadn't said it. Why, he wondered with annoyance, had he popped off like that anyway? What he wanted was a job with the Bantams, and he was certain he could hold down the first sack well enough to suit most managers. Therefore, why had he made the virtual admission that fielding bored him? He didn't know, but he let his breath out with relief when Mercer said, "If you'd still like to hook up with the Bantams, I'll give you a fair trial. I can use more power on my batting list, and if the sample you showed me today stands up, I can probably hand you a contract."

"I'll take a whirl at it," said Marty.

Mercer studied him for a careful moment. Marty tried to read behind the other's eyes, but couldn't. Mercer asked, "Bender Shane's your brother, isn't he?"

"Why, yes," admitted Marty guardedly.

"You're pointing toward the big time, aren't you?"

"Of course."

"In that event, how come your brother didn't farm you out?"

Marty wisely checked an impulse to say it was none of Mercer's business. He said slowly, "I didn't want his help. I want to prove I can make the grade alone."

"It means a lot to you?"

Marty nodded. "Yes," he said, "it does."

Ever so slightly Mercer's eyelids drooped as if to hide an expression he could not control. Marty felt something tighten up inside him as he watched the manager.

"That's fine," said Mercer as he turned away.

"Now what the deuce?" Marty muttered to himself. "I've got to watch that guy."

# CHAPTER 4

Whatever premonitions Marty might have had concerning Mercer did not last long. Or, rather, they were not permitted to take on definite form because of more active matters demanding his attention.

Mercer seemed to have forgotten him at the moment. So had the other Bantams. Marty stood around while the interrupted workout got under way again. He didn't mind being ignored just now because he had a few important matters to mull over in his mind.

To start with, he accepted the fact he had committed himself to a baseball career. He would have to take the business as seriously as he could and face the thing with logic. He must keep one elementary fact foremost in his mind, namely that he'd have to make good with a minor league club before he could ever expect the majors to recognize him.

Well, he'd picked his team—the Bantams. Maybe he'd picked a bad apple. He didn't know, but time would tell. He was merely going on the theory that a rookie would have a wider chance on an independent club than on a farm club. If he caught fire on the Bantams, almost any of the major outfits might try to buy him.

But first of all he'd have to establish himself with the Bantams, and he had sense enough to know he'd have to establish himself as someone the men would want on their team, not only as a slugger but as a guy to tie to. The latter was important. It meant that Marty Shane would have to watch his step, would have to start acting and thinking like a minor leaguer, rather than as part owner of the big league Quakers. It would never do for him to show his distaste for the Bantams' training camp, as opposed to the comparative luxury of the Quakers' layout down in Florida.

Having decided to be big and tolerant about it all, he felt a glow of righteousness. He was still in that benign mood when Mercer called the practice to an end. The manager strolled over to Marty Shane and asked, "Have you found a place to stay?"

"Not yet."

Mercer thought for a moment, then said, "Dinty Mead's got a big room to himself. I'll put you in with him." He turned and called, "Hey, Dinty!"

Dinty Mead turned out to be the shortstop who had made wisecracks when Marty was batting. Marty watched him carefully, trying to keep resentment from his eyes. Dinty's face was noncommittal. They shook hands perfunctorily when Mercer introduced them.

"I'm sending Marty over to bunk with you," said Mercer.

"Okay," said Dinty briefly. Then to Marty, "I'll be with you as soon as I take a shower."

He went into the low, flat, paintless building that served the Bantams as a locker room. He came out before any of the others, proving he had not kept Marty waiting longer than necessary. Marty chalked it up in Dinty's favor.

When they started from the field they had some unobtrusive company. The youngster who had acted as Marty's guide was keeping abreast of them at a respectful distance. He was eyeing Marty with great respect.

"Hi, William," Marty said.

William's grin stretched wide. He was very proud to be thus recognized.

"You sure socked that ol' apple, Mr. Shane," William said.

"Thanks, William."

"Yes *sir,* you sure lambasted it."

"I was lucky," Marty said.

"No, *sir!* 'Twasn't luck. You're good!"

Marty, slightly embarrassed, turned to Dinty. "My public," Marty said.

Dinty said, "Yeah," and let it go at that.

The conversation died, but William escorted them all the way, quite content to stare at Marty with admiring eyes.

The room was in a private home. It was an improvement, Marty suspected, over the accommodations of the local hotel. He learned later that the men, although living in different houses, all ate at the same boardinghouse. He also found that the room he was to share with Dinty Mead was large and pleasant, with two beds and ample space. When the two men entered Marty said, "Not bad. Darn nice in fact."

Dinty uttered another noncommittal "Yeah."

He was a smaller man than Marty, compact in build and quick of motion. His hair was sandy and rebellious. So were his eyebrows. His eyes, a lively blue, had the quality of striking their targets hard in passing, of absorbing what there was to learn in one quick thrust. There was a puckish air to his tilted features, a capacity for deviltry, yet also a capacity for sober thought. As if to make up for his abruptness, Dinty said, "My stuff's all over the place, but don't let that fool you. There's plenty of room. I'll clean out a couple of these bureau drawers."

"Thanks," said Marty, feeling slightly ill at ease and not knowing exactly why. He sensed something important in this guy, Dinty Mead, an undercurrent of restless strength. To make conversation, Marty remarked tentatively, "The Bantams've got themselves a nice layout down here."

"Who you kiddin'?" demanded Dinty.

It pulled Marty up short, but he recovered neatly.

"Myself, maybe," he admitted.

Considering this, Dinty Mead approved it. He nodded slowly and said, "Kiddin' yourself is okay, up to a certain point. The question is, are you kidding yourself beyond that point?"

He was clearing the bureau drawers while Marty opened his suitcase on one of the small beds and started to unpack.

"I'll bite," said Marty. "What's the answer?"

"The answer is, don't kid yourself the Bantams are a soft touch. Don't kid yourself that you can tear 'em wide apart. A lot of college guys have tried, and failed."

Marty stopped unpacking and turned around, his diplomacy suddenly worn thin.

"What're you driving at?" he demanded bluntly.

Dinty turned too, leaning against the bureau. His eyes were probing, but impersonal. He said, "Keep your shirt on. I'm trying to steer you right."

Marty stared a moment longer, then found his resentment dwindling. He finally said with frank astonishment, "I believe you are. Why?"

Dinty shrugged. "We've got to room together for one thing, and I don't want to be hooked up with a guy who gets off on the wrong foot. Besides, I'm not bragging when I say I know the ropes. Baseball, in fact, is about all I *do* know. I've come up through the sand lots and the semi-pros. I'm aiming for the top as well as you."

"What makes you think I might get off on the wrong foot?" demanded Marty curiously.

"The cards, to start with, are stacked against you. Did you know that?"

"Well—no, I guess I didn't. Why are they stacked against me?"

"If the guys don't already know, they soon *will* know who you are. That you're Bender Shane's brother, and that you own a slice of the Quakers."

Marty had a hunch about what Dinty Mead was

driving at, but he wanted to hear the other put it into words. So Marty asked, "What's wrong with that?"

"The guys you'll be tied up with from now on," explained Dinty patiently, "are pros, not amateurs. They're out to make a living. It's bread and butter to 'em and that's something you'll never have to worry about. The fellows'll know that, and you can see how it's liable to affect them unless you watch your step."

Marty nodded slowly. "Sure," he said. "I get it. I'll try to keep my neck pulled in. And—thanks."

"There's part of it you probably don't get yet," Dinty went on slowly, "unless you happen to know the background. It's about Lobo Mercer."

Marty's interest quickened. "What about Lobo Mercer?" he demanded.

Dinty took his time. He said at last, "I don't know why I'm shootin' off my mouth like this, except that I think you ought to have the break of knowing what you're up against."

He ran a hand through his hair and went on. "Lobo's a fine baseball manager. Don't ever make a mistake about that. He turns out good teams. The trouble is, he's got a sour spot in him. He's convinced he was bounced out of the majors before he was through as a catcher. That may be true. There are a lot of rumors as to *why* he was bounced, but none of 'em are backed up by fact. He played with the Quakers, and your brother was the guy who bounced him."

"Huh?" The word jerked out of Marty Shane as if someone had jabbed him with a pin.

"Yeah, that's right. And Mercer's had his knife out for Bender ever since. It's no secret. Mercer makes no bones about it."

"Well, I'll be hanged," breathed Marty.

"You'd better be *careful* too," warned Dinty.

"I will."

"It's almost time to eat," said Dinty. "Let's go. You can get settled later."

"Okay. How's the chow?"

"So-so." Dinty grinned. "But don't expect too much of good old Southern cooking."

The Bantams ran their training table in a huge old house which, in the past, had undoubtedly been referred to as a mansion. The six Doric columns across the front still towered in gloomy dignity as if resentful of the noisy Yankees who passed between them. The fine old home had obviously seen better days and was unhappy in its present role.

Most of the first-string Bantams lived there. It was their clubhouse and they referred to it as such. The huge, high-ceilinged living room could accommodate them all in their leisure moments. It was shabbily but adequately furnished. There was a big round table at one end for cards.

Dinty led Marty to the dining room and found places for them at one of the two long tables. Marty was ill at ease, more so than he would have cared to admit, but he soon found that no one paid him much attention. He was still a rookie.

He was glad when the meal was over. Most of the men moved to the living room, but Marty had no desire to join them. He felt uncomfortably alone. He started back to his own room, mildly surprised that Dinty Mead came with him rather than hanging around with the other guys. Marty had the feeling that Dinty sensed his loneliness and was trying to keep him company in an offhand, unobtrusive way. Dinty said, "I read detective stories. I'm a sucker for 'em. I got a guy locked up with a time bomb. His hands and feet are tied, and he's tryin' to take the bomb apart with his teeth. I gotta see if he can do it. I'm afraid he can't."

"Two to one he makes it," offered Marty.

"Well, I hope so," said Dinty wistfully. "He's a pretty good detective. I'd hate to see him splattered all over the wallpaper."

Back in their room, Dinty buried his nose in the mystery magazine while Marty finished his unpacking. A short time later Dinty said, "He did it. What a guy!"

"I figured he had a chance," said Marty. He turned toward the bureau with a handful of socks, then stopped abruptly at the sight of a big figure in the doorway. Dinty saw him too and said, "Hi, Jake. Come on in. Shake hands with Marty Shane. Marty, meet Jake Larkin. He's got a room in this house too, and Lobo thinks he can teach the big hick to pitch."

Jake Larkin moved into the room. He was tall, rawboned, and his joints were limber, as if hinged with rubber. He looked awkward, but Marty didn't let it fool him. He sensed the effortless, complete control behind Jake's languid movements. Marty's own hand, big as it was, was lost in Jake's huge palm when they shook hands. Marty had the uncomfortable sensation that Jake could have pulverized his bones if he'd wanted to bear down, but Jake took it easy. He said, "Pleased to meetcha," and looked as if he meant it.

Marty liked him right away. He studied Jake's long craggy face, the mild blue eyes, and decided promptly that Jake Larkin was deceptive in appearance; that the average man could make the big mistake of considering Jake Larkin slightly dumb, could mistake his slow deliberation and his outward shyness for stupidity. Marty sensed, however, that what Jake lacked in formal education was more than balanced by an ability to reason clearly, and to find a deep contentment and amusement in the things about him. Marty said, "A pitcher, huh? My natural enemy."

"Aw, shucks," said Jake. "I ain't a pitcher yet. All I can do is chuck 'em at the catcher. I got a lot to learn."

"All he can do," said Dinty dryly, "is to hit a dime at sixty feet. When he learns to bend 'em, I hope I'm batting somewhere in a different league. Care if I tell Marty how Lobo discovered you?"

"Well, no," said Jake. "Not if you make it short and tell the truth." He ambled over to a chair and sat down, giving the effect of unhinging himself.

"It happened this way," Dinty said. "Lobo and a couple of friends were huntin' rabbits one day last fall up in Vermont. They were working through a big field of shocked corn, kicking each shock as they came to it to scare out any rabbits that might be hidin' there.

"Pretty soon they found this guy Jake Larkin wandering around in the same field. Jake had a rabbit hung on his belt, but the funny part was, he wasn't carrying a gun. Lobo noticed this and asked him where he got the rabbit. Jake looked surprised and said, 'I throw rocks at 'em.'

"Lobo was smart enough not to call Jake a liar right to his face, because Lobo knew something about a Vermonter's so-called sense of humor, so

Lobo said, 'Well, son, that's mighty interesting. How about joining us for a while so we can see how you do it?'

"Jake said, 'All right,' as if he didn't know he was being kidded. He reached in his pocket and brought out a couple of stones about the size of pullet eggs. He passed up a pair of corn shocks, and when they asked him why, he said, 'There ain't no rabbits in 'em.' "

Dinty turned to Jake and demanded, "Am I right so far?"

"Yeah," said Jake. Then, by way of explanation, he added, "I got a feelin' for such things. Somethin' just tells me where the rabbits are."

"Very logical," said Dinty dryly, then continued with his narrative. "Jake finally found a shock that suited him. He gave it a couple of kicks, and sure enough, out come a rabbit. Jake let fire with the first stone. He missed with that one, but Lobo swears the stone traveled so fast he couldn't see it. He only saw where it kicked up dirt a couple of inches from the rabbit. The rabbit jumped straight up in the air, and when he hit the ground again Jake nailed him with the second stone. Killed him dead. That right, Jake?"

"Yeah," admitted Jake, embarrassed. "But it was an easy shot, and I was mighty lucky. I ain't really as good as that. I only get about one out of every ten I shoot at."

Marty's intuition told him that he was being taken for a fancy buggy ride, but stronger than this was a fantastic hunch that there was a sound element of truth in the weird yarn. There was something about Jake's calm assurance which made it seem plausible that he could do exactly what Dinty claimed of him. So Marty moved his head in a conservative nod and kept his face straight.

Jake, sensing the strain on Marty Shane's credulity, explained anxiously, "You see, I've always liked to throw things at targets. I been doin' it since I could pick up a stone. It was a hobby, I guess, but I never knew it was worth anything until Mr. Mercer got all excited when I knocked over the rabbit. He seemed to think I was pretty good and wanted me to leave the farm and play baseball for him. I told him I'd rather stay with my cows, pigs, and horses, but when he came back next day and handed me a baseball, a nice new smooth baseball, I was lost."

"How come?" asked Marty, hoping he wasn't sticking out his neck for the punch line.

But Jake appeared still eager to make Marty understand. Scratching his ear thoughtfully, Jake said, "It was the feel of the baseball that got me. It was exactly right, you see, for throwing. The best thing I'd found up to that time was the Kiefer pear. They ain't much good for eatin', but they're firm and solid and a good size. They couldn't stack up with a baseball, though." Jake's eyes lighted fondly at the mere thought of the smooth horsehide in his hand. "Mr. Mercer had a catcher's mitt with him, and after I'd thrown a few into the mitt, he was more excited than ever. He said he'd give me five hundred dollars to come down here, so I said I would. But," he hastened to add, "it was only because I liked to throw a baseball."

And Marty believed him, believed him without the slightest doubt, sensing that Jake Larkin was indeed an amazing person. And Marty received immediate proof that Jake was even more amazing. He absorbed the shock with a quick intake of breath when he saw a small, gray, furry head emerge from the pocket of Jake's coat. Marty stared in frozen wonder when a sleek gray squirrel emerged, climbed calmly up Jake's coat, and settled on his shoulder.

"Hey, Dinty, do you see it *too*?" demanded Marty hoarsely.

"Oh, sure," said Dinty reassuringly. "That's Hannibal."

"Well, I'll be hanged," breathed Marty.

"I like animals," said Jake apologetically. "And

they seem to like me. You see, I get sort of lonesome for the farm, so I have to have a few pets." He produced a peanut and gave it to the squirrel. Hannibal cracked it solemnly, extracted a nut, and munched it daintily, holding it between his tiny paws.

Dinty told Marty, "You'll get used to it. All the cats and dogs in town follow him around. He's got a small menagerie out in the back yard, but our landlady, Mrs. Hopkins, lets him get away with it because she likes animals too."

"That reminds me," said Jake, getting carefully to his feet in order not to disturb Hannibal. "Gertrude ain't feelin' so good. I better go see how she's makin' out."

"Gertrude," explained Dinty, "is a pig. So long, Jake."

"So long," said Jake, ambling out the door.

"Quite a guy," said Dinty when he'd left.

"I like him," said Marty promptly.

"So do I. And he'll be one of the great pitchers in history if he doesn't get too homesick for the farm—and go back to it."

# CHAPTER 5

Next day Marty joined the Bantams for their morning workout. The reserve in their attitudes toward him proved they all knew who he was by this time, that he was part owner of the Quakers. He caught them sending speculative looks in his direction, looks that challenged him to shoot his mouth off or to make some indication of amusement, some gesture of superiority to suggest he didn't have to play baseball unless he wanted to. They were challenging him silently to prove he had a right to be there, a challenge Marty Shane accepted.

He watched his step with all the care at his command. He kept his mouth shut and his eyes upon the ball. Lobo Mercer treated him as impersonally as he might have treated any other rookie, an attitude which suited Marty.

He showed up well again in batting practice. He plastered some boomers to the outfield while the Bantams looked on, reserving comment. He also had a chance at fielding practice, but not the sort of chance he'd hoped for. He had told Mercer that his position was first base, but Mercer, ignoring this, sent Marty to the outfield to chase flies. Maybe Mercer needed outfielders more than he needed first basemen. It worried Marty because he didn't kid himself at all about his ability to catch flies. He was no good at it, and he knew it. He couldn't judge them properly.

He was jumpy and uncertain when he took his place in right field. Mercer was boosting the fungos to the outfield. He looped one to left, then to center, and then it was Marty's turn.

When he saw the ball leave Mercer's bat, he had the panicky feeling that he ought to do something about it, either come in or move back, but not knowing which way to move he did the next best thing and stood still. Luckily the ball came almost directly to him. He had to take only a few quick forward steps to catch it. It burned his hand, warning him of the tenseness of his muscles.

Catching the first ball didn't improve his morale too much, because he knew he lacked the elements of a good outfielder, the quick instinct that tells an experienced man where the ball is coming, the sixth sense that should set a fielder's feet in motion at the crack of the bat.

Marty didn't have it. He had to study the flight of the ball for several precious instants while he tried to see it as something other than a white spot in the sky. There was no way for him to tell, until the ball was well upon its way, whether it would land behind him or in front of him.

He was perspiring freely from sheer nervousness when Mercer sent the next ball at him. It wasn't a setup like the first one. Marty watched it tensely until it reached the top of its arc. He decided he'd have to come in for it, but when he had taken a few steps toward the plate he saw with alarm that he'd misjudged it.

He plowed to a halt and backtracked desperately, finally managing to get under the ball in the nick of time. It banged hard against his mitt again, but he hung on to it. He felt no sense of accomplishment, knowing that any mediocre fielder could have caught the fly in his hip pocket.

His third and final effort was a magnificent example of how *not* to play the outfield. When the ball left Mercer's bat it looked like a high looper. Marty came racing in, only to find that the ball had no intention of coming down where he had hoped it would. It remained suspended in the sky.

Marty jerked to a stop again, and started to back-pedal as he'd done before. This time, however, a world's record in running backward wouldn't have helped him much. He increased his efforts mightily, but the added surge of power brought nothing but disaster.

The spikes of his right shoe caught in a chunk of turf and down he went. He landed in a sitting posture, bounced painfully several times, then skidded to a stop flat on his back. He heard the thud of the ball a few yards behind his head. He would have been grateful at the moment for a nice dark hole to crawl into, but he had to get up instead, go chase the ball, and heave it to the plate.

The Bantams had enjoyed the show. Some of them were still doubled up with laughter. Marty Shane felt like a first-class fool. His face was red and his spirits were dragging in the dust when he obeyed the disgusted wave of Mercer's arm and started for the plate.

When he was there, Mercer said, "I could get you a bicycle and a bushel basket if you think they'd be of any help."

51

"Not even a long pole with a net on it would help," said Marty miserably. "I simply can't judge flies, not long ones."

"You're telling *me*," said Mercer, and let it go at that.

Marty expected to have the shirt razzed off him at lunch time, but nothing of the sort happened. No mention was made of the unhappy incident, proving more conclusively than ever that the men were still determined to hold him at a distance.

Marty didn't let that worry him so much just now. He was more concerned as to how the brilliant exhibition of outfielding might affect his chances of making the squad. Maybe, he reasoned miserably, Mercer had had no idea of letting him play first base to start with, but after Marty's gruesome display of fielding during morning practice there was no chance at all that Mercer would ever again trust him in the orchard.

However, things looked a little brighter during the afternoon session. Mercer let him hold down first base awhile, and Marty only muffed one grounder, a grasscutter anyone might have muffed. All in all he felt as if he'd put on a pretty good fielding show, even though he had sense enough to know that the Bantams' regular first sacker, the old veteran Wally Gant, had a rhythmic knack of covering the bag which Marty Shane could probably never match. Old Gant, however, had lost his batting eye, and the rumor was his legs were going fast.

Nevertheless, it was something else for Marty to worry about. Much as he wanted to hack himself a spot on the Bantam club, he encountered an unsuspected soft streak in himself which made him dislike the idea of trampling too hard on someone else's toes. Wally Gant was a great guy, one of the greatest who'd ever come down from the big time.

Marty talked it over with Dinty Mead that evening in their room. He said, "Look, Dinty, I'm going after that first sack job with everything I've got. I may land it on my batting average—I don't know. But if I *do* land it, I'm going to feel like a first-class heel for nosing out old Wally Gant."

"You're still not a pro at heart," said Dinty bluntly. "It's dog eat dog in this business, with not much room for noble motives. You gotta be tough, Marty."

"Sorry I mentioned it," said Marty stiffly.

Dinty grinned. "I'm glad you brought it up. It's nothing to be ashamed of, and it just so happens I can put you straight."

"Go ahead," said Marty, still slightly huffed.

"Wally's probably pullin' for you stronger than anyone else."

"Huh?" jerked Marty in surprise. "Come again."

"Wally Gant's been smart. He's one of the few big timers who has saved his dough. He's stuck it away in the old sock, bought himself a farm, and now he wants to live on it."

"Why doesn't he?"

"Wally and Lobo are close friends. Wally's been sticking around to help Lobo out until Lobo can find someone to take his place. You might be the fair-haired boy."

"If I am," said Marty with relief, "I'll feel a lot easier in my mind about it."

"Frankly," admitted Dinty, "I guess I'd feel the same. Well, I got to catch up on my reading. I've left a guy hangin' from a rope tied to his ankles. He's hangin' from a tree and his head's only six inches above black scummy water of an Everglades swamp. The swamp is filled with hungry alligators. One of 'em is about to grab him. I think he's a goner."

"Why," demanded Marty curiously, "do you leave 'em in such fixes? Why do you quit reading at that point?"

"I like to take time to figure how they can get out of the jams," admitted Dinty. "But this guy hasn't got a chance."

"Two to one he makes it," offered Marty.

"Quit spoilin' my fun," Dinty snarled at him. He cocked his feet on the bed, opened the magazine, and read avidly for several minutes. He finally let his breath out gradually, admitting, "The gator didn't get him. What a guy! Here's what he did. He . . ."

A knock sounded on the door. Dinty muttered with annoyance, then yelled, "Come in!"

A big man entered. He wasn't fat but he looked soft, slightly doughy from inertia. He moved as if he hated exercise, yet there was vast assurance to his walk. He entered the room as if he owned it. His face was florid, and its surface blandness was refuted by his eyes, which were sardonic, green, and bold. His clothes bagged carelessly upon him and his gray felt hat was sweat-stained, shapeless.

He flapped a meaty hand and said, "Hi, Dinty. I smell news—fine succulent material for my public."

Dinty tossed his magazine upon the bed, placed the tips of his fingers together, and stared thoughtfully into space. "My big moment," he breathed raptly. Then, "I was born of poor but honest parents. Got that? My first toy was a baseball—a pitiful, ragged baseball with broken seams. I loved that baseball. I kept it under my pillow nights. It made a big dent in my head, of course. I still have it. The dent, I mean. Want to see it?"

"Backstage for you, son, backstage." The visitor brushed him off. "You're a fine shortstop with a future, but your past is drab and dreary. In contrast I refer you to your roommate, Mr. Shane. He's got the sort of past that interests me. Mystery, glamour. And, incidentally, I haven't had the pleasure of meeting Mr. Shane."

"Oh," said Dinty, looking hurt, "so that's why you're here. I never would have guessed it. What delayed you? Marty, meet Rudy Kemp. The *Buffalo Blade* sends him down here on a vacation to keep an eye on us. He's supposed to be a baseball expert. He writes a column."

Marty shook hands with Kemp and was sure he didn't like the man.

Kemp said, "I came to interview you, Marty," his tone suggesting he was doing Marty Shane a favor.

"Go ahead," said Marty.

"How come you picked the Bantams for a tryout?"

"I had to start somewhere."

"I'll accept that. But why did you decide to start at all? As part owner of the Quakers, you don't have to play baseball for a living. May I tell my public that you felt the surge of baseball fever in your blood? That you experienced the fierce urge to keep the family tradition alive?"

56

"Why do you have to tell them anything?" demanded Marty shortly.

"Come, come, man, be cooperative," Kemp urged sharply. "You're a public figure now. Or if you're not, I certainly can make one of you."

Marty was certain by this time that he didn't like the guy.

"Look, mister," said Marty evenly. "When I want your help I'll ask for it."

Glancing at Dinty, Kemp made a resigned gesture which, in effect, said, "This guy's a dope. He doesn't know who I am. He doesn't recognize opportunity when he sees it. I'll have to be patient with him."

Aloud, Kemp said, "Look, Marty, I've got a living to make, even if you haven't. You're hot copy, kid, and I've got to use you. Gimme a little straight info now. Why aren't you playing on one of your brother's farm teams?"

"Try and guess," snapped Marty.

"Okay," said Kemp, a hard note creeping into his voice. "Maybe I *can* guess. Sport writers aren't dumb, Marty. Word gets around, and the word is that you and your brother aren't exactly pals. Could it be, then, that he refuses to farm you out, and that you've decided to show him anyway? Could that be it, Marty?"

Marty shot a glance at Dinty who, behind

57

Kemp's back, was making calming gestures. Marty didn't heed them. Kemp, by this time, was under his skin like a tick. Marty's voice was brittle when he said, "I've decided I don't like you, so don't push your luck too far. You can guess whatever you please, Kemp, but be *very* careful what you write. Just leave my brother out of it, or I might decide to smack your teeth in."

"I think you'd be too smart for that," Kemp told him shrewdly.

"Not the way I feel right now," said Marty.

Kemp shrugged his flabby shoulders. "Okay, son," he said with resignation. "If that's the way you want it. Too bad we can't be friends."

"I like it this way," Marty told him bluntly. "And don't slam the door when you go out. My nerves are bad."

Starting for the door, Kemp said, "You only *think* they're bad. You ain't seen nothin' yet."

He was careful, however, not to slam the door. When he had left, Dinty said disgustedly, "Of all the knuckle-brained saps I ever saw, you win the Swiss cheese bat."

Marty, though still sore, had gained a respect for Dinty Mead, which tempered his anger now. He said apologetically, "But confound it, Dinty, that guy Kemp's a louse."

"Sure he is," conceded Dinty. "So what? He's

top baseball writer for your hometown team—if you make the team. The local fans eat up his stuff. Even the Bantams think he's hot. Or, if they don't, they're not dumb enough to say so. The guy swings weight."

Marty was beginning to sweat a little. He didn't even attempt bravado. He was getting a new slant on the matter now that his temper had cooled. He admitted grimly, "Maybe I hit into a double play."

"No maybe about it," said Dinty flatly. "You've still got a lot of things to learn, and playing ball with the scribes is one of them. Rudy Kemp will scorch your pants, but plenty."

"I'll bat his ears down," declared Marty with a return of spirit.

Dinty picked up his magazine with the resigned air of a man who'd done everything he could.

Marty Shane said grudgingly, "Okay, I'll try to watch my step."

"You'd better," Dinty said from behind his magazine.

# CHAPTER 6

In the following days Marty tried to stick to his resolve. He was a good boy. He kept the zipper fastened on his uncomfortably tight coat of humbleness. He felt the strain, however, because it wasn't the sort of apparel to which he was accustomed.

He was puzzled, too. Having accepted the fact that Lobo Mercer was getting him nice and fat for some sort of a barbecue, he found it hard to accept Mercer's attitude of friendliness. It even reached the point where Marty began to believe he might have been wrong in his suspicions, and there were times when he actually had to restrain himself from liking Mercer.

Finally, as a compromise, he tried to place a sensible interpretation on the matter. He decided Mercer was smart enough to know a good thing when he saw one, namely that Marty Shane was an apple-buster whom any team would be glad to own, and that if Mercer wanted to own him, which he obviously did, it was to Mercer's advantage to keep Marty in the proper frame of mind.

The explanation suited Marty at any rate, and received endorsement from Mercer's attitude of tolerance toward Marty's occasional fielding blunders. Mercer shrugged them off good-naturedly, with the air of a man who knew he couldn't have the moon.

The other Bantams didn't follow Mercer's lead with too much eagerness, but their early distrust of Marty Shane seemed to be dying out, and, in a reserved sort of way, Marty got along pretty well with most of them. The outstanding exception was Mugger Blain, who made no secret of his dislike for Marty. The matter came to a head in a practice game, the first game in which Marty had been allowed to play. He was on the second squad, with Blain on the mound pitching against the regulars.

Mugger Blain, as usual, was in a grim mood. He had made no progress toward resigning himself to the obscurity of a minor league pitcher. He still figured himself big time, and had to prove it with every throw he made.

And, to give the man credit, he was proving it satisfactorily that day. He had the regulars swinging themselves out of joint. They squeezed across one unearned run in the seventh, the fault of the rookie backstop, Frankie Pell, who was behind the plate for the second team.

With a man on third, Pell tried to pick him off and threw wide. The run came in, and Blain hit the roof. He told Pell what he thought of him in no uncertain terms, and the kid, red-eared, stood there and took it. He didn't have much choice, because he too was hoping for a contract, and he didn't want to whittle down his chances by making an enemy of an important guy like Blain. Marty sympathized with Pell, but could understand that the rookie was using his head.

The run broke a scoreless tie to put the regulars into the lead, 1–0. The second stringers hadn't had much luck up to this point against the sidearm deliveries of the first string hurler, Andy Mark. Mark appeared to be in midseason shape, and had held the second team to five scattered hits, one of which had been chalked up by Marty Shane.

Mugger Blain retired the side without further damage, but when he came in to the bench at the end of the seventh inning he was in an ugly frame of mind, and he didn't care who knew it.

"I want that run back," he told his teammates harshly. "And you'd better get it for me."

The lead-off man, Joe Tilden, the second baseman, did his best. He smacked a hard grounder to Dinty Mead at short, but Dinty came up with it smoothly and made the out at first.

The right fielder, Hap Carson, did a little better. He connected with the third delivery for a nice single to right field.

Jim Winters, the center fielder, was the third man to face Mark in the top of the eighth. The hit-and-run sign was on for the first pitch. Mark must have suspected something of the sort, because he threw the first one wide on the outside. Winters, however, faithful to instructions, went over after it and had the good luck to get his bat on it. It was a dribbling grounder down toward first. Mark streaked across to field it, but Carson was well on his way toward second, so Mark wisely made the out at first. With two down and a man on second, Marty Shane came to the plate.

A hit at this point would bring in a run to tie the score, and Marty wanted that hit as badly as he had ever wanted one in his life. He wanted it for himself, not for Mugger Blain. He stepped to the plate and shook his muscles loose.

He took the first pitch for a called strike, but he didn't let it worry him. The second offering was a wide hook which went for a ball. The third one was a trifle high, for another ball. Mark was showing his respect for Marty Shane, trying to keep his deliveries where Marty wouldn't murder them.

The fourth pitch was another hook, but Marty figured it to break across the pan, so he took a cut at it. He connected solidly but a little late. It was a line drive just outside the first base foul line, so close to being fair that it probably raised a rash of goose pimples on Mark's hide.

With a two-two count Mark was overcautious on his fifth pitch. It sank in below Marty's knees for the third ball, thereby putting the pitcher in a spot. Mark took plenty of time in serving up the payoff ball. Maybe he took too much time. It was a fast hook across the letters, and Marty bopped it on the nose for a howling single over short. Carson scored, and Marty held at first, feeling mighty pleased with himself. He had a hard time keeping his expression casual.

Andy Mark tightened up and struck out the next man to retire the side. But the score was tied, and the regulars were grim as they took their turns at bat in the bottom of the eighth.

But Mugger Blain, finding himself back in the ball game once more, was poison to the men who faced him. He set them down in order, and the score was still sewed up in the top of the ninth. The second stringers tried to salt the game away, but Mark tied them up in knots. The score was still 1–1 when the regulars came up in the bottom of the ninth.

Blain appeared to have everything under control in the first stages of the inning. He struck out the lead-off man, and the second batter popped out to third.

Things didn't look so bright, however, when the next two batters rapped out a pair of husky bingles to put men on first and third. The fifth hitter stepped to the plate determined to be a hero if he could. Marty moved away from the bag, and the runner took a lead.

Blain toed the slab, raised his arms, and let them drop upon his chest as he looked the runners over. He faced the batter, then lifted his left elbow about three inches from his body. Marty didn't see the movement of the elbow. He should have spotted it at once, because it was a prearranged signal between him and Blain. Marty Shane, as a result, was caught flat-footed when Blain whirled and threw to first.

Marty made a fine effort, a swift wild leap, but the ball bounced off the padded end of his mitt. He scrambled for it desperately but couldn't get his hand on it in time. The man came in from third with the winning run. The game was over.

Marty's first reaction was that Blain had crossed him up. Then common sense told him Blain would not have cut his own throat in that manner. Marty knew he must have missed the signal. He wished the ground would open wide and swallow him.

Mugger Blain stood for a long moment with hands upon his hips, a tableau of sizzling outrage. Then he roared, "You feather-brained bush leaguer! What're you doing in a baseball uniform? If you want to take a nap you ought to wear pajamas. Or maybe you let that run come in on purpose." He strode toward first base, planted himself in front of Marty, stuck out his ugly face and yelled, "I ought to bust you in the nose!"

Marty's temper swooped up like a skyrocket, but he held on to it desperately. To start with, he knew he was in the wrong, and that knowledge was the only thing that kept his fist from colliding with the open target of Blain's jaw. It was a terrible temptation.

He felt the color draining from his face, for he had never staged a greater battle with himself. He forced himself to remember he was still on probation with the Bantams, that a brawl with Blain might wind him up for good. He clung fiercely to the thought that baseball was the only thing that mattered now, that slugging Blain was less important than the big league goal he'd set himself. With an effort, he admitted hoarsely, "Sorry, Blain, I didn't catch your sign."

Blain spat in the dirt, just missing Marty's toe. Marty's muscles twitched, but he managed to hang on. Blain turned contemptuously away and started from the field.

Most of the Bantams were still staring at Marty Shane. When he swung his eyes to meet them, they let their gazes slide away from him. Marty didn't get it right away, then it hit him like a ton of pig iron.

He'd guessed wrong again. He should have slugged it out with Blain. The Bantams thought now that Blain had scared him green. Marty started after Blain but checked himself. He'd missed the boat and had sense enough to know it. He admitted it to Dinty Mead that night.

"Yeah, Marty," said Dinty thoughtfully. "You probably should have nailed him, even though he probably would have knocked the tar out of you."

"Says who?" demanded Marty.

"No offense," said Dinty hastily. "But Mugger had a few pro fights in the ring before he turned to baseball. He wasn't going anywhere as a fighter, of course, but after all, a pro's a pro."

"I've had some ring experience too," Marty pointed out.

Dinty nodded slowly, trying not to appear doubtful of Marty's chances against Blain. "You might have flattened him," conceded Dinty. "And if you had, or even if you hadn't, I think it would have been a good thing for you to have taken a crack at him, because the guys don't like Mugger. They respect him for what he's done," he added fairly, "and for what he still can do. But most of 'em, I think, are also scared of him. I'll admit *I* wouldn't want to tangle with him." He hesitated a moment, then said, "The fact is, Marty, the boys've been sort of hoping you *would* tangle with him, because they figure you're the only one with size enough to have a chance against him. I guess that's why they acted disappointed today."

"Well, now," said Marty, brightening, "maybe I can give 'em what they want."

"Maybe you can, but don't go lookin' for it. Wait till Mugger gives you another chance."

"I'll wait."

"You may have to wait a long time."

"Why?"

"Lobo bawled the hide off of Mugger for shootin' off his mouth at you and Pell today. Mugger's smart. He knows Lobo means business."

"Mugger'll slip up again."

68

"Sure he will," conceded Dinty.

"I hope it's soon."

But it wasn't soon, and Marty found the job of waiting definitely unpleasant. To make it worse, Rudy Kemp got in his first pot shot a few days later. Local papers reached the Bantams through the mail. Dinty Mead showed one of them to Marty. It was folded at the sport page. Pointing to Kemp's column, Dinty said, "Your pal's started to sound off. Read it, son, and don't say I didn't warn you."

Marty read it. The part dealing with him said: "There's a rookie down here by the name of Shane, Marty Shane. You guessed it, Bender's brother. Young Shane got tough when I tried to interview him. Don't ask me why. Maybe he thinks the minor leagues ain't fittin' for 'im. Maybe he's ashamed to be hooked up with one, seeing he owns a quarter interest in the Quakers. He's a good hit, no field first sacker. He swings a good club, but picks daisies in the garden. Maybe Lobo'll sign him up. I couldn't say. Lobo is all hush-hush on the subject."

Marty said through his teeth, "The louse!"

"Yeah," conceded Dinty. "Old poison pen stuff. There'll be more of it."

"And I've got to sit and swallow it?"

"No, you don't," said Dinty. "You can bat Kemp's teeth in if you want to and get yourself kicked off the club. Lobo'll do it, because he's scared of Kemp. I'm sorry, Marty, plenty sorry, but I don't like the way things are shaping up."

"Let's have it straight."

"Okay, fella, here she is. Kemp's got a toe hold on the hometown fans. If he peddles the idea you're no good, they'll believe him. Then if Lobo signs you up, they'll be sore. Lobo knows all this, and it's a question in my mind whether or not he'll take the chance. He knows where his dough comes from—the fans."

"So that's the angle, huh?"

"It is from where *I* sit."

Marty's face was hard, his anger gone. "I'll sweat it out," he said.

Dinty nodded, "Yeah," he said. "I thought you would. And more power to you."

# CHAPTER 7

Sweating it out was worse than sweating out the taut moments before an air battle with Japanese Zeros. Marty had done that too, and he preferred it to the sustained torture of fighting an almost hopeless battle for a contract with the Bantams.

There were times when he wondered why he didn't pack his grip and leave. He was wasting his time here, despite the fact that he was belting the horsehide to all corners of the state and fielding as well, if no better, than he had always fielded. Yeah, he ought to pack his duds and head for home. But something held him, something he couldn't over-come, an inherent stubbornness which wouldn't let him quit, even though he had the setup all figured out.

He figured it this way: Lobo Mercer was out to settle his grudge, fancied or otherwise, against Bender Shane, and he was obviously trying to settle it through the medium of Marty Shane. The process was not complicated, as Marty saw it. The idea was to keep Marty on the hook as long as possible before dumping him with a "Sorry, Shane, but I've decided you aren't good enough for the Bantams."

That was it, all right, because several of the rookies, including Jake Larkin, had already been handed contracts, while others had been dropped from the squad. Marty Shane was the only likely prospect whom Mercer was still keeping on the griddle.

Marty didn't take it calmly. He boiled inside like a thermal spring, although his exterior control was masterful. He had too much stiff-necked pride to permit Mercer or the Bantams to suspect the licking he was taking. He intended to restrain himself until the final moment. Then when no more hope was left, he intended to indulge himself in one colossal popping of his safety valve. He would not fold his tent and leave the Bantams meekly. He'd leave like a tornado.

Having settled all this in his own mind he began to feel better. He didn't know quite why except that, by nature, he was neither a sourpuss nor a confirmed pessimist. His natural instincts were to enjoy life, a process which he found, to his surprise, was not impossible even at the moment, despite the turmoil in his mind.

For one thing, he liked baseball, liked it with every fiber of his being. It had taken a firm grip on him at last, and the daily workouts were a pleasure for him. He could almost forget his troubles during the hours he spent upon the diamond.

And it wasn't as bad as it might have been when he was off the diamond. A close friendship had developed between him and Dinty Mead. He had also taken a great liking to the amiable Jake Larkin. So had Dinty, and the liking seemed to be reciprocated by the rookie pitcher. The three of them spent a lot of time together, and Marty soon became accustomed to Jake's assorted pets.

Furthermore, Marty's relations with the other Bantams were not as strained as they might have been. Things seemed to be easing up a trifle. This may have been because Mugger Blain made no further attempt to call a showdown with him, and the Bantams may have figured that Blain himself was not too eager for a brawl with Marty.

At any rate, things weren't so bad, and Marty

found himself coasting along from day to day without much effort. And if his own faith in himself took too great a slump, there was always William who had obviously selected Marty as his hero. He trailed Marty like a faithful spaniel, eager to run errands or to be of service when he could. Marty became fond of William, and knew he would miss the youngster when the Bantams broke up camp.

The reporter, Rudy Kemp, continued to get in Marty's hair. Kemp seldom wrote a column without including a nasty dig at Marty Shane. It was a deliberate campaign to keep Marty's stock as low as possible, and it undoubtedly had some effect among the Bantams.

And to make things worse, Rudy Kemp was always hanging around, giving the impression of a lazy hound dog sniffing about for news. He showed up at almost all the workouts, spreading himself listlessly in the shade of the nearest pine tree, usually with a fat cigar sticking out of his loose mouth.

At such times Marty had to exercise a lot of will power to keep from walking over, booting Kemp to his feet, then taking him apart. The force of the urge began to worry Marty, because he couldn't throw it off. The mere sight of Kemp did something dangerous to him. He didn't like the feeling. It scared him. He began to feel that his pride, even his sanity, demanded some act of retribution toward the man who was kicking him around so much in print. He was getting away with murder, and he shouldn't be allowed to.

The plan he finally grabbed at was a feeble sort of plan. Even Marty thought so. But he knew he had to do something on short notice, something to take the pressure off himself, something more or less aggressive which might prove to Kemp that Marty Shane had no intention of being kicked around like a soccer ball without doing something in return. Having reluctantly discarded the pleasant notion of slapping Kemp around a bit, Marty decided to go ahead with his idea, weak as it was, of competing against Kemp in a war of nerves.

Marty had a camera, a small speed one for which he'd paid a lot of money. He considered himself an amateur photographer of sorts, but didn't take the thing too seriously. It was the thought of the camera, coupled with the unlovely picture of Kemp sprawling in the shade, which gave him his idea.

He brought the camera with him next time he came to practice, and sure enough, Rudy Kemp, as if coached for the part, ambled over to his accustomed spot beneath the tree, lit his cigar, and stretched out on the ground. Marty walked over to him.

Kemp eyed Marty with sardonic interest and said, "Hello, Marty. Have you finally figured out that it pays to be friendly with me?"

"Well," said Marty easily, "I don't think I'd put it quite that strong, but I will say that you've aroused my artistic instinct."

Kemp's green eyes narrowed watchfully. He was flat on his back, but he stretched his arms back beneath his head to prop it up for a better look at the man standing over him.

Kemp said, "Don't try to be funny, kid. You're not the type."

"I wouldn't think of mixing art with humor," Marty said.

"What're you driving at?"

"I was just thinking what a fine picture you make lying there, what an excellent study of an alert reporter covering his assignment. And then I began to wonder what your editor would think of your alertness, how pleased he'd be with your fireball methods of collecting news." Marty stepped a few paces to the right and went on, "Now, for instance, if I only had a camera, I could get a fine shot of your energetic figure with the players in the background to show that you really *are* on the job."

"Go away," sighed Kemp. "You're getting tiresome."

"You don't even have to move," said Marty, beginning to believe he was making a fool of himself, and that his plan was quite as flimsy as he'd believed it. He decided to play it out, however, so he reached in his hip pocket, brought out the camera, and started to adjust it.

The result was instantaneous and highly gratifying to Marty Shane, who had scarcely dared to hope that he could prod Kemp in a weak spot. But obviously he had. Obviously Kemp possessed an unsuspected pride in his profession. Either that, or he was scared of losing a soft job.

At any rate, Kemp let out an alarmed snort and came off the ground with the heaving motions of a terrified cow. He was panting from exertion, thoroughly outraged.

"You're forcing your luck, Shane," he rasped.

Marty grinned, then admitted, "It was more luck than I expected, and not very good luck for you. Was it, Rudy? Maybe you won't be taking any more naps out here again. Maybe I might have my camera with me, and maybe I might get a nice clear shot. It's a very good camera, Rudy."

Kemp thought this over swiftly and didn't like it.

"I'll burn the shirt right off your back," he snarled, resorting to the only threat he knew, one that had never failed. him yet in dealing with a professional athlete.

But it failed him this time. Marty laughed at him

and said, "Don't try to be funny, *kid*. You're not the type."

Kemp chewed savagely on his cigar, trying to think of a verbal blast that would whittle Marty down to his proper size. But before he could form his thoughts into words, another voice put in a claim for immediate attention.

The voice said, "Ba-a-a-a!"

Both men whirled toward the sound, and both men froze to respectful immobility at the sight of a rangy, rawboned billy goat who had stopped some twenty feet away, and was regarding them with baleful, calculating eyes.

Marty recognized the newcomer with uncomfortable alarm. It was Geronimo, one of Jake Larkin's pets, a word which could be applied to Geronimo only in his relations to Jake himself. Geronimo loved Jake, as all animals did, but so far as anyone else had been able to determine, Geronimo's hatred for the balance of mankind was uncompromising and inclusive.

Geronimo had gone out of his way to prove this on so many occasions that Jake finally had been forced to keep him tied, under the threat that Geronimo would otherwise end up in the form of very tough goat meat. Geronimo didn't like to be tied up, and spent most of his waking hours trying to solve the mystery of his tether.

Apparently he'd solved it, had accomplished a Houdini, and was now in search of his beloved master. Apparently, too, the futility of the search thus far had frayed his nerves to the breaking point, placing him in a humor which, even for Geronimo, was evil. He was looking for someone to dispute his right of passage, and had reached the point where he intended to make an issue of it.

This much was clear, to Marty at any rate, who had no intention in the world of placing any obstacles, least of all himself, in Geronimo's path. Unfortunately, however, both he and Kemp were spotted directly in Geronimo's line of march, and Geronimo appeared to be deciding, at this time, which target was the more desirable.

His glittering blue eyes swung back and forth from Kemp to Marty. The tension of the moment swelled and built up pressure. Marty, trying not to call attention to himself, stood immobile as a post. He slid a glance at Kemp, and was glad to see that the reporter wasn't enjoying himself either. Apprehensive sweat was trickling down Kemp's face. He was trying to stand still, but his jowl quivered.

He then did a very stupid thing which appeared to be an attempt to prove to Marty that Rudy Kemp possessed stern fiber which could not be intimidated by a moth-eaten goat.

Kemp said with loud authority, "Get out of here, Geronimo! G'wan, scram!"

That did it. It settled Geronimo's vacillating thoughts to the point where he was no longer an animal of indecision. He made up his mind at last, and concentrated his entire malignant attention upon Kemp.

Marty breathed easier and began to enjoy himself. Kemp breathed louder and did not enjoy himself. The wicked gleam in Geronimo's eyes became intensified. He looked almost happy as he studied Kemp with merciless intentness as if working out a plan of strategy.

Kemp tried to outstare him, but fell far short in his endeavor. Kemp's breath began to whistle as he breathed. The color left his face, leaving it the shade of putty. Geronimo, as if prolonging the delightful moment, took several mincing steps in Kemp's direction. Kemp's nerve snapped like an overstrained violin string. He whirled about and started to run.

Geronimo uncorked his battle cry, a loud, glad "Ba-a-a-a!" Sand spurted backward from his hoofs as he went into his charge.

Marty started to run too, carried high upon a wave of inspiration. Instinct told him he would never have another chance like this again. He ran parallel with Geronimo, adjusting his camera as he ran.

The final instant of the drama was delayed beyond the point of logic. There was no reason to believe that anyone built like Rudy Kemp could cover ground in such astounding fashion. It is true he'd probably never *had* to cover ground that fast before, but, even so, it was an amazing exhibition.

His form was awful. His legs were stiff and his arms made motions like a man slapping at a swarm of bees. His head was pulled back between his shoulders, and his big feet hit the ground with loud percussions. However, what he lacked in form was compensated for by indomitable spirit and determination; also by the fact that Geronimo meant business. Kemp's cigar was still clamped firmly in his teeth.

Geronimo, however, was merely toying with him. The old goat seemed to have the instincts of an actor. He had the center of the stage now. Everyone was watching him, yelling loud encouragement.

So he delayed the climax of his big dramatic moment until his victim was approaching second base. Then with a splendid surge of speed he flashed in for the kill.

It was a masterful bit of work, as nicely timed and executed as a triple play. No goat without experience could have pulled it off like that, could have nailed Kemp on his broad posterior while Kemp was in the middle of a stride.

The result was definitely spectacular. Kemp left the ground in a smooth arc. He stayed in the air a surprising length of time before crashing in a nose dive directly upon second base. Geronimo squared off for another go, but Jake Larkin reached the scene just in time to restrain his gentle pet with a sharp command.

Geronimo let out a happy "Ba-a-a!" of recognition, trotted to Jake, looked up at him with fond blue eyes; then, like a kitten, he rubbed against Jake's legs.

Kemp, meanwhile, had pulled himself together in a dazed sort of way and was sitting on second base. The cigar, what was left of it, was still in his mouth. It had come in violent contact with the bag, and was spread about the lower portion of his face like a mouthful of dry leaves. Marty took another picture of him, just in case the first shot wasn't good.

The Bantams had enjoyed the show tremendously. They stood in a grinning circle around Kemp, who wasn't enjoying himself at all. However, he spat out the remnants of his cigar, climbed stiffly to his feet, and made the best of it.

"Well, boys," he said. "I've had my workout for

the day. Hope you enjoyed it. Glad to oblige you any time."

He started from the field but pulled up short when he came abreast of Jake Larkin and the now harmless Geronimo. Kemp glared at Jake and said, "Next time I'll brain the dumb brute with a baseball bat."

"Why didn't you brain him this time?" Jake asked mildly.

"Because I didn't have the bat," Kemp alibied.

Geronimo said, "Ba-a-a-a!" It had a derisive sound because it had been timed so neatly.

A couple of the Bantams guffawed their appreciation. It was more than Kemp could take. He lost his head in a surge of crazy anger. One of the men near him held a bat. Kemp snatched it swiftly and made a lunge for the unsuspecting Geronimo.

But Kemp never had the chance to use the bat. Jake's long arm shot out with the speed of one of his fast balls. It landed, open-palmed, against Kemp's face, already tender from its contact with second base. Kemp staggered back, let out a curse of pain, and dropped the bat.

Jake picked it up and said, "Don't ever make a pass at any of my pets again. You got off lucky this time."

Kemp hauled in a deep breath to pull himself together. His eyes were mean as they rested upon

Jake. Jake met the gaze, his own eyes hard and filled with deep dislike. Kemp finally said, "Most rookies have a lot to learn."

"I'm learnin', and I pick my own school books."

"Okay," Kemp answered softly, shrugged and walked away.

Marty moved over to Jake and said, "Welcome, pal. You're in my club. I felt lonesome. Now Rudy's after your hide too."

Jake grinned and said, "It's a good club, Marty."

"Yeah. Exclusive. But maybe we won't have to take it lying down."

"How come?"

Marty patted the small bulk of the camera which he had returned to his pocket. "My secret weapon," he said mysteriously. "I'll let you know how things develop—and I *mean* develop."

# CHAPTER 8

When the workout ended, Marty took a fast shower, climbed into his clothes, and headed for the business section of Pine Mound. His small convoy was, as usual, on the job. Marty asked him, "William, do you know of any place in town that develops pictures?"

"We got a movie house," said William helpfully.

"That's not exactly what I had in mind," said Marty. "I don't want to look at pictures, I want some developed from camera film."

William scratched his head and came up with the

right answer. "There's a man in town who takes pictures. Mr. Perkins."

"Okay," Marty said. "Let's go find Mr. Perkins."

Mr. Perkins turned out to be a professional photographer. He was a small, bald-headed man, and helpful. His studio was above the hardware store.

"Why, sure," he said. "I'll be glad to help you out. If you want to wait, I'll develop them right away."

Marty said he'd wait, and a short time later Mr. Perkins came out with the damp prints. He was smiling with amusement, but when he spoke to Marty his voice carried a note of professional respect.

"These are excellent snapshots, young man. Excellent."

"Both of them?" asked Marty anxiously.

"Oh, yes, indeed. Particularly the action shot. It's beautiful, both in technique and—ah—subject matter."

He handed the prints to Marty, who scanned them eagerly, particularly the one featuring Geronimo. It was, as Mr. Perkins had proclaimed, a beautiful piece of work. The shutter had been snapped at exactly the right instant, just as Geronimo had made forceful contact with his target and had started Kemp upon his flight. Marty grinned with satisfaction.

"How," asked Mr. Perkins, "did you manage such an excellent shot?"

"I'm afraid," admitted Marty, "it was mostly luck. I was traveling on the dead run when I made the exposure, so I didn't have time to use the finder. Yes, I was pretty lucky."

"Under those conditions," admitted Mr. Perkins, some of the former respect absent from his tone, "a picture of that sort is no less than a miracle. But then, many of the most spectacular snapshots are accidental."

"True enough," said Marty. "And I'm mighty grateful for *this* accident. Thanks a lot for helping me, Mr. Perkins. What do I owe you?"

"Twenty-five cents."

Marty paid him, then hurried back to his room. He found Dinty and Jake already there.

Dinty was saying, "And the guy's locked up in the same cage with a wild gorilla. The gorilla can't quite reach him because the gorilla's got on a big collar, and there's a rope through the collar which is tied to the side of the cage. But the gorilla's chewin' on the rope, and in another couple of bites he'll have it broken. Then, of course—"

"To be continued in the next installment," Marty interrupted. "Let the monkey chew on the rope while you boys chew on this."

He showed them his prize picture. They stared at it in astounded, flattering silence.

Dinty finally muttered hoarsely, "It's a fake. It can't be true."

"It's true enough," said Marty. "I got in a lucky shot."

Jake said, "I ain't seen anything like that since Mabel, my Rhode Island Red, laid a square egg."

Dinty was grinning broadly now. So was Jake. Dinty said, his voice awe-filled, "It's dynamite. You've got Rudy where you want him now."

"I want to be on hand when Rudy gets a look at this," said Jake. "I wish he were here."

It was almost as if Jake had rubbed a magic lamp. A voice from the doorway said, "He *is* here." They all turned. It was Kemp.

"Gosh," said Jake, "I'm gettin' good."

The reporter had regained his poise. He said, "I seem to remember that you snapped a picture of me, Marty, while I was sitting on second base."

"That's right," admitted Marty cautiously.

Kemp nodded toward the picture Marty was holding. "You didn't waste any time having it developed. How did it turn out?"

"Fair," said Marty.

"I'll buy it from you. How much?"

"Not for sale."

"Let's see it."

Marty handed him the print—the one starring Geronimo. Kemp looked at it and grunted as if someone had jabbed him in the solar plexus. Beads of sweat came out upon his forehead as he stared at the snapshot. His hand shook slightly.

"I didn't know you'd taken *this* one," he said thickly. "Will you sell me the negative?"

"No."

"Do—do you intend to send this picture up to Buffalo?"

"What do *you* think?"

Thinking, at the moment, seemed to be a painful process for Rudy Kemp. Venom and apprehension were struggling for supremacy in his expression.

And Marty, as he watched Kemp's struggle, felt his own sense of values becoming tangled. According to all the elements of justice Marty realized he should be getting great satisfaction from the moment. It puzzled him to find his elation wavering, going stale. It didn't make any sense at all.

It made a great deal *less* sense when he reached into the pocket of his shirt, produced the negatives for both pictures, and handed them to Kemp.

"Here, take the things," he growled.

And not until the negatives left his fingers did Marty Shane begin to understand why he had made such an outrageous move. The understanding reached him first through an unaccountable feeling of cleanliness, almost as if he'd just scrubbed off a layer of heavy dirt. There was also a new feeling in his lungs. They seemed more flexible, able to accept more breath. He filled them now, with satisfaction, and the air felt good.

Kemp snatched the negatives with greedy fingers. He too breathed deeply, steadying himself. A look of triumph colored with contempt formed in his eyes. His poise came rushing back. He asked, "Just why did you do that?"

"Because," said Marty promptly, "you're a rat. If I kept those negatives and held them over you, I'd be as big a rat as you are. It's not my way of paying off a debt."

"You're a fool," said Kemp with deep conviction.

"I'd rather be in that class than in yours. Now beat it."

But Kemp didn't beat it right away. He studied Marty shrewdly before asking, "Are you expecting me to do you favors now?"

"Get out!" said Marty tautly. "Get out, worm, before I step on you!"

Kemp took the hint this time. When he had gone, Dinty groaned. "Of all the mush-brained fielding plays I ever saw, you just turned in the prize. You had him a mile off first base, and you let him get back to the bag. Do you think we ought to have his brain examined, Jake?"

Jake thought it over carefully and said, "Well, no. I guess his brain's all right. If you fight a guy like Rudy with his own weapons, you're draggin' yourself right down to his level."

This time Dinty Mead took time to think things over. "Yeah," he admitted finally. "I guess I wouldn't feel too good about it either. It's too much like blackmail. It's a good racket for Rudy, but not for Marty." He changed the subject. "You've got a letter over there on the dresser, Marty."

Marty opened the letter, read it, and said quietly, "I'm going to buy a plane."

His two friends whirled and stared at him. "A *what?*" demanded Dinty.

"A flying machine," said Marty. "They're here to stay. Hadn't you heard?"

Dinty eased himself into a chair. "But what do *you* want with one?" he asked weakly.

Marty shrugged and said, "I've got over two thousand hours in Mustangs, and I'm homesick for the air. This letter's from a friend of mine who gives me the chance to buy a little crate. It's almost new, a two-place cabin job with a hundred and twenty horsepower motor. It's a sweet little crate, a Cloudbuster, and it's got a low landing speed. I could bring it down out here on our baseball field with plenty of space to spare."

"Sounds like fun," admitted Dinty. "But have you given a thought to the Bantams? What they'll think?"

"Yes," said Marty. "And I've decided I don't care what they think. They haven't given me a tumble yet anyway, so they might as well be convinced I'm a bloated plutocrat. Furthermore, my chances of getting a contract out of Mercer are about one in a million. Also, if I don't buy this crate now, I'll lose the chance and may never get another bargain like it. So I'm going to buy it."

So Marty bought it, and got quick delivery. His friend flew it in a couple of days later, and found ample landing space upon the baseball field. He took Marty up at once, and not until they'd left the ground did Marty realize how much he'd actually missed the air. His nerves relaxed. It was an excellent tonic.

He accustomed himself in a few minutes to the feel of the controls, finding the Cloudbuster to be an honest little crate, well-mannered and responsive. Its modern safety factors made it almost foolproof, which suited Marty fine. He was ready now to take things easy. He'd spent enough time in hot ships like the Mustang. When he brought it down to a gentle landing, he was highly satisfied with his new possession. Through previous inquiries he had spotted an airport near Columbia, just a short hop from Pine Mound, where he could buy high octane gas and get service for his plane.

The Bantams as a whole were interested in the Cloudbuster, but their reactions were more or less noncommittal. Most of them probably disapproved of such a display of wealth. Marty had hoped to bring them to a more tolerant way of thinking by taking them up for joy rides. It was a good idea, but Lobo Mercer promptly spiked it. He forbade the Bantams to take hops with Marty under threat of being booted off the team. Obviously Lobo Mercer was not air-minded. Either that, or he had a deeper motive, the determination to keep Marty Shane hanging on a hook.

He was still hanging on the hook when the Newark Jays paid a visit to the Bantams. It was an annual event, this preseason game between the Bantams and the Jays, made practical by the fact that the Jays' training camp was also in South Carolina, not a great distance from Pine Mound. The two clubs exchanged visits on alternate years, and the game had gradually become a contest of considerable importance. Even a superstitious significance had taken root to the effect that the winner of this game would start the season with a hatful of luck. The Bantams took it seriously. So did the Jays. Both teams usually shot the works.

Marty felt some of the pregame excitement creeping into his own bones, even though he was not officially a member of the Bantams. He had the feeling he was hot; that if Lobo Mercer gave him a chance against the Jays, he could show enough stuff to make things very uncomfortable for Mercer—in the event Mercer had decided not to sign him up.

But when Mercer announced the starting lineup, Marty Shane was on the bench. Wally Gant, the veteran, was stationed at first base. Marty watched the game get under way with stony eyes.

# CHAPTER 9

The Bantam lineup was packed with its first stringers. Mugger Blain was on the mound. Blain, of late, had been showing a lot of his old-time stuff, but there was some doubt that he had reached the point where he could go the entire distance. The point wasn't faraway, but Marty didn't believe Blain could last nine innings unless the going was particularly easy.

It wasn't. The Jays had a hitting team this year. They were pretty ragged in the field, but their manager was gambling that the weight of the Jays' bats could overbalance their consistent ball-juggling. He was gambling upon batting as opposed to fielding skill.

The Jays forced Mugger Blain to pour it on right from the start. They were dangerous, and Blain had sense enough to know it. He pitched to every man, and held them scoreless for the first four innings.

The Jays had a rangy southpaw on the mound by the name of Artie King. King was good, a definite big league prospect, and he showed his stuff today. He held the Bantams to three scattered hits in the first four innings, and the game went into the fifth a scoreless tie.

Blain ran into a little trouble with the first two men. A pair of short singles put Jays on first and second. Blain took a hitch in his pants. He struck out the next two men, but the next Jay got his bat on a low hook and sent it for a single. A run came in. The next man flied out to short right, but the Jays were in the lead.

King blanked the Bantams in their half of the fifth inning. Mugger Blain got away to a strong start in the top of the sixth. He struck out the first man, and retired the second on an infield fly to Dinty Mead. The third Jay, however, brought disaster to the Bantams.

He connected solidly with the first pitch, slamming a savage grounder back to Mugger Blain.

Blain bent to field it, but the ball took a mean hop and cracked against the shinbone of his right leg. Then it caromed toward the first base foul line. Wally Gant raced in to cover it, but the sudden demand on his aged legs was more than they could take. He pulled up lame, with a strained muscle in his right leg. Cal Steuben, the catcher, recovered the ball in time to hold the runner at second base.

It was a tough break for the Bantams—two casualties on a single play. Blain wasn't badly hurt, but his leg was still numb from the blow, and Mercer took him out of the game. Gant had to go too, limping badly.

Marty Shane was honestly sorry for Wally Gant, but he couldn't help hoping that the accident would give him the chance he'd wanted. It did. Mercer sent him in to cover first, and, to everyone's surprise, sent Jake Larkin in to pitch.

Jake had developed fast, but there was still a big question as to whether the rookie was ready to be tossed into a game of this importance. He was still wild and uncertain with his hook, though deadly with his placements.

It appeared, however, that Lobo Mercer knew what he was doing. Jake strode to the mound as unconcernedly as though he were going out to the barn to milk a cow. His warm-up pitches were smooth and hard. He seemed completely undisturbed and confident, the ideal temperament for a pitcher.

Mercer's strategy became evident as soon as the first batter faced Jake Larkin. Jake threw nothing but straight balls, but they went in like bullets exactly to the spots Cal Steuben called for, and Steuben knew the likes and dislikes of most of the Jay batters. The present batter collected one weak foul and two called strikes, thereby contributing the third out.

The bottom of the sixth inning was uneventful. So was the entire seventh inning, with the exception of Jake Larkin's superb speed and control. He had the Jays blinking stupidly at the ball as it fizzed past them.

In the top of the eighth, however, the Jays began swinging at Jake's offerings. One Jay connected with a rattling single over second, which didn't seem to bother Jake at all. He pitched calmly and methodically to retire the side.

The Bantams were a little jittery as they came to bat in their half of the eighth. The Jays' one-run lead began to look pretty big, because King was still going strong.

Kip Jurgen, center fielder, was lead-off man for the Bantams. He waited out a full count, then clipped the money-ball for a hard grounder down to short. The shortstop bobbled it and drew an error. Jurgen reached first, and Joe Peel, left fielder, came to bat. He laid down a bunt along the third base line. It was intended as a sacrifice bunt, but was so beautifully executed that Peel had enough speed to beat it out. With men on first and second and no outs, things began to look brighter for the Bantams.

But not for long. Cal Steuben flied out to left field. Okie Gordon, third baseman, looped a high foul which the Jays' first baseman gobbled up.

It was a nice spot for Marty Shane—or a bad one, depending on how you looked at it. A hit at this time would be worth a million dollars. That part was good. But if he failed to hit, he'd be a mug. That part was bad.

Marty thought about these things and then forgot them, centering his entire attention on the pitcher. He'd had a chance to study King, whereas King had had no chance to study him. King must have thought of this, because he seemed a little nervous. He undoubtedly knew Marty's reputation as a slugger.

He tried to sneak in a fireball for the first strike. It came sizzling in just above the knees, and Marty liked them there. He took a full swing and connected solidly.

He knew he'd tagged that one as he headed down for first. He saw the center fielder running, saw him make a wild leap and knock the ball to earth. The Jay himself came back to earth off balance. He tumbled on his back, and Marty dug in for second.

The third base coach held him on the keystone sack, which suited Marty perfectly because two runs had scored ahead of him. The score was now 2–1, with the Bantams in the lead, and Marty was feeling pretty fine about it.

He would have felt even better if one of the following Bantam batters had given him a chance to score, but King pulled himself together and retired the side with two strike-outs and a fly ball.

The Jays were grim and dangerous when they came to bat in the top of the ninth. There was a businesslike air about them, as if they knew what they were doing. And obviously they did.

They had tumbled to the fact that Jake Larkin was pitching nothing but straight balls. He was, of course, placing them with deadly accuracy, but when a batter doesn't have to worry about a curve, his frame of mind is apt to change.

It was that way with the Jays, at any rate. The lead-off man cracked a sharp single over first. The second man sacrificed him down to second with a bunt, which Jake fielded handily and got to Marty in time.

The third Jay slammed a single over third, but

Joe Peel came in fast to field it on the first bounce. He whipped the ball to the plate in time to cut off the runner who had already rounded third. The runner scrambled back to the bag and slid in ahead of Steuben's throw. The other Jay runner went to second.

Lobo Mercer pulled Jake from the game at this point, but Jake was still calm and unperturbed in the knowledge that he'd done exactly what had been asked of him. He'd pitched according to instructions, and had done a perfect job in that respect.

Mercer sent a left-hander, Jerry Gill, to try to check the batting spree. Gill deliberately walked the fourth Jay in order to fill the bases and set up a double play.

Things looked brighter when the next batter went out on an infield fly to Okie Gordon. If Jerry Gill could struggle past the next man at the plate, the ball game would be in the bag. The catch was that the batter, Murphy, was the Jays' cleanup man, the most dangerous slugger on the team.

Murphy proved it on the first pitch, which was supposed to slide off the outside corner of the plate but didn't. Murphy socked it, blasted it square upon the nose. The ball left his bat in a low white streak, heading between first and second.

Marty Shane was playing wide, but he didn't see

that it would help him much. It looked like a hope-less try, but Marty made the effort. He drove with two short strides, then left the ground in an ex-plosive leap. He flattened his body in the air, and shot his gloved hand toward the ball.

He felt a violent blow against his mitt. He hit the ground with jarring force. Dust gritted in his teeth. He lay there for a moment, almost stunned. Then gradually it dawned on him he'd made the catch. The ball was still embedded in his glove. The game was over.

He scrambled to his feet, trying not to look as bewildered as he felt. He'd just made an incredible fielding play—he who was supposed to be a duffer at the art. He was as much surprised as any of the others, but he tried hard not to show it.

In fact he tried too hard, for when the Bantams surrounded him, loud in their exuberance, he made a fool of himself. Instead of admitting he'd made a lucky stop, which they all knew anyway, he tried to pass it off as a commonplace event like shaving, tried to appear nonchalant as if he could make such catches any time he wanted to.

It was the wrong approach. The Bantams didn't fall for it. They had been ready to laugh *with* Marty over the fantastic miracle, ready to enjoy its hu-morous aspects; but when Marty missed the chance to belittle his own effort, it put a different slant on things. The eyes of the Bantams grew unfriendly. Cal Steuben said, "I think he's about ready for a possum hunt."

Joe Peel agreed. "Yeah. He hadn't ought to leave the South without baggin' at least *one* possum. How about it, Marty? Would you like to go on a possum hunt?"

Marty realized by this time how badly he'd bungled his opportunity. Instead of gaining a toe hold in the Bantams' esteem, he was right back where he'd started from. They were needling him now, working up to some sort of gag. Well, he'd asked for it, and the least he could do was to go along with the gag. Either that or take an even deeper slump in their estimations. He tried to tell himself he didn't care *what* they thought of him, but he couldn't make it stick. So he answered dully, "Sure, I'd like to bag a possum."

"Fine," said Peel with relish. "We'll organize a hunt tonight. Good time for it. No moon, clear sky. There ought to be lots of possums in the woods. Come to the clubhouse at eight o'clock."

"All right," said Marty. "I'll be there."

"Wear old clothes," Steuben warned.

"Okay."

After their showers, Marty, Dinty, and Jake

walked home together. Each man seemed concerned with his own thoughts, and the conversation was sporadic.

Marty, in an effort to lift himself from his own gloom, said: "Cheer up, Jake. They knocked you out of the box. So what? It probably won't be the last time, and besides it wasn't your fault today. You did exactly what they told you to. You chucked the apple dead center into Cal's mitt every time. It was a fine pitching exhibition, and you kept your head all the way through."

"Yeah," admitted Jake. "But just the same it ain't a very good feeling to get your hat knocked off on your first start. I wish they'd let me try a few curves."

"Your curves aren't ready yet," put in Dinty. "They're coming along fine, and in a few more weeks you'll have 'em under control. You'll have a bend to 'em like a boomerang. You did fine today, so quit worrying."

"Can't I worry just a *little*?" Jake asked plaintively.

"No," said Dinty flatly. "Let Marty take care of the worrying. He's got something to worry about."

"You're telling *me*," growled Marty. "I sure made a chump out of myself today. I knew that catch was nothing but a miracle, and so did everyone else. But I couldn't let it go at that. Not Marty

Shane. I had to pretend I'd done it on purpose."

"Anybody might have done the same thing," said Dinty. "The trouble was that you were playing against a bad setup. You got any ideas on this possum hunt?" he asked cautiously.

"I'd be a dope if I *didn't* have," said Marty. "The Bantams have figured me for a swelled head all along, and now I've proved it to 'em. It's pretty obvious they've got their own system for dealing with rookies who begin to think they're good, and the possum hunt is part of the treatment. It's probably nothing but a new angle to the old snipe hunt where they give some sucker a bag, and tell him to hold it while they shoo the snipes into it. Then everybody goes back home and leaves the poor chump there all night. You probably know the angles, Dinty, but I don't want you to tip me off. It's my show. I asked for it."

"Fair enough," said Dinty, and let it go at that.

# CHAPTER 10

Marty showed up at the clubhouse promptly at eight o'clock. He was wearing a sweatshirt, a pair of old pants, and a pair of durable shoes. He suspected he'd have to do a lot of walking before morning. He had also slipped a small pencil flashlight in his pocket.

The hunting party was limited to four Bantams beside himself: Cal Steuben, Joe Peel, Okie Gordon, and Swede Hansen. They all piled into Cal Steuben's car and started out. Their only equipment consisted of several heavy burlap sacks and flashlights. Everyone, with the exception of Marty, was in an amiable frame of mind. Marty made no attempt to pretend he was interested in the expedition. He held his tongue and let the others do the talking.

Cal Steuben, acting as master of ceremonies, asked, "Know anything about possums, Marty?"

"No."

"Well, they're funny animals; got funny habits. You probably wonder why we don't need dogs or guns to catch 'em. It's this way. They sleep all day and come out at night, generally start prowling about nine or ten o'clock. The trick is to locate one just before he wakes up, because they seem to sleep sounder at that time. A lot of them, you know, hang by their tails from a small branch while they're sleepin', and these are the ones we try to find."

He paused, waiting for some comment from Marty, but Marty remained silent, letting Steuben continue with his fairy tale.

"Well," Steuben went on undiscouraged, "when we find one hanging by his tail, we have to use what's called a possum whistle. It's a whistle tuned so high that the human ear can't hear it, but a possum can hear it and it scares the daylights out of him. It scares him so much he lets go with his

107

tail, but by that time someone is standing underneath him with the bag. He drops in the bag, and we got 'im.'"

"And I suppose you'll let me hold the bag," said Marty.

"Of course, Marty," said Steuben heartily. "That's why we brought you out. We'll give you a chance at the first one."

"I can hardly wait," said Marty.

There wasn't much conversation from then on. Cal Steuben was busy with his driving. They were soon out of town. They left the main highway almost at once, and began following narrow sandy roads which twisted through the dense pine woods. Steuben stopped the car every now and then as if trying to decide which new road to follow, but he always appeared to recognize the landmarks with a grunt of satisfaction. He drove as if he knew where he was going.

Marty tried with all his concentration to remember the various turns Cal Steuben took, but soon gave it up as hopeless, because all the forks in the road looked alike to Marty in the glare of the car's headlights. He also tried to cling to his sense of direction which ordinarily was pretty good; but it was helpless now. He was soon completely lost, which, he reflected grimly, was just the condition of befuddlement the Bantams were trying to build up in him.

When they finally stopped, it seemed to Marty that they must be miles and miles from home. The others jumped from the car with the air of eager huntsmen, but Marty climbed out with less enthusiasm, wondering how soon they'd run away and leave him.

To all appearances they had no intention of doing it right away, and Marty was even slightly puzzled by their attitudes. Either they were putting on a good act, or they were actually excited over the prospect of finding a possum. Peel distributed the bags, and the four Bantams headed into the woods with an eagerness which suggested they had forgotten about Marty Shane. Marty shrugged in mild bewilderment, but followed the illumination of their flashlights before he became engulfed in darkness.

Cal Steuben carried a powerful five-battery torch, with which he swept the lower branches of the trees. They walked for some distance, and the walking was not easy. Dead pine needles formed a slippery carpet on the ground. Marty was soon lost again, without the foggiest notion of where they had left Cal Steuben's car.

The men began to show impatience. Swede Hansen grumbled, "What's wrong with the dopey little fools? Don't they know we're lookin' for 'em? We ought to have found one by *this* time. Maybe Marty's a jinx."

The words had scarcely left Swede's lips when Steuben came to a sudden halt and said in a strained, taut whisper, "There's one now!" He snapped off his powerful torch and whispered, "Give me a weaker one. This searchlight might wake 'im up."

He took Peel's smaller torch and played it cautiously upward. Sure enough, there was the possum, an ugly, long-snouted little animal, hanging limply by its tail.

Marty stared at it, his emotions badly tangled. He knew there was *some* sort of catch to this possum hunt, but he was being forced to the reluctant belief that the hunt, up to this point, was authentic. It was hard to doubt the tense satisfaction of the men around him. And he *had* to believe the evidence of his own eyes, because the possum was right there for him to see.

So when Steuben said, "Okay, Marty, get ready!" Marty cast aside his doubts and decided to enjoy himself, for the moment at any rate. He found his hands trembling slightly as he opened his bag and moved beneath the possum.

Steuben said hoarsely, "Okay, Swede, gimme the whistle." There was a moment's silence. Then, "Hurry up, Swede. Let's have it."

More silence. Then Swede's voice, worried and apologetic, "I—I was *sure* I had it, Cal. But—but it doesn't seem to be here. I guess I left it in my other pants."

"Why, you dumb cluck!" raged Steuben. "You— you—" He checked himself, breathed loudly through his nose, and pulled himself together. When he spoke again, his voice, though reasonably calm, was filled with disgust. "Okay," he said. "So you forgot it. But we can't leave that possum hanging there." He thought a minute, ran his light along the limb of the tree, then said: "We can still get 'im. Marty'll have to do the muscle work because he's a rookie. Now look, Marty. We'll boost you up to the first branches of the tree; then you can crawl out that big limb to where you can reach the small limb the possum's hanging on. Then you can slide your bag under him and jolt 'im loose. Snap into it before he decides to wake up."

Marty needed no further urging. He was filled, by this time, with the spirit of the chase. He wanted to bag a possum, and the opportunity was here. He hurried to the trunk of the tree, stuffing the bag under his sweatshirt as he went. Strong hands grabbed his legs and heaved him upward. His hands closed upon a limb, and a moment later he was astride it.

Cal Steuben, manipulating the flashlight from the ground, rationed the light sparingly to Marty, giving him just enough to permit his cautious progress along the branch toward the dangling possum. When he reached the small branch upon which the possum hung, he pulled the bag from beneath his sweatshirt. He was working himself into a position where he could slip the bag up over the unconscious animal when the flashlight in Steuben's hand went dark.

Marty waited a moment, then whispered hoarsely, "Gimme some more light."

No answer. Marty's nerves gave a warning jump as he heard the padded sound of feet upon the carpet of pine needles down below. The sounds receded. The Bantams were slipping away into the night.

Marty yanked in his breath for an angry bellow of protest, but he caught himself in time and let his breath out silently, determined not to give them the satisfaction of knowing he was peeved.

But he was—mad enough to chew the limb in half with his bare teeth. When the first wave of fury had subsided, however, he realized with some surprise that the anger had been directed almost entirely against himself. He'd let them make a fool of him after all. They'd put their act across, and Marty Shane had fallen for it like a moron.

Nevertheless, as he straddled the limb in the utter darkness, he was forced to admit that the act had been a dandy. They'd pulled it off like professionals. He even gave them grudging credit for it, and the humor of his predicament stretched his lips into a reluctant grin.

"You really *are* out on a limb, son," he told himself.

He then tackled more practical angles of his predicament. The possum, after all, was still there, and Marty was just stubborn enough to want to finish the job he'd started. He'd take the animal back to them and toss it in their laps.

But even as he fumbled for his tiny pencil flashlight he began to have belated premonitions. He began to doubt the nocturnal habits of the possum, began to doubt that any animal in the world could sleep suspended by its tail.

The weak beam of his torch confirmed the doubt. The light showed clearly that the possum's tail was tied firmly to the small branch. He reached out an experimental finger, poked the hanging body gingerly, and found it to be a moth-eaten specimen of taxidermy. The thing was stuffed.

He told himself, "You're a very bright boy, Marty. Very bright."

He also reminded himself once more that he had asked for it, and that he might as well see it through. He decided to take the stuffed possum back to its owners, in tacit admission that he'd fallen for the gag, and that he harbored no hard feelings. So he untied the cord which held the tail, and heard the body thump upon the ground.

Descending the tree in the pitch darkness wasn't easy. He was also perspiring more profusely than the effort warranted, a fact which brought him to the frank conclusion he was definitely nervous. It annoyed him. He gave himself a fight talk.

He was lost. So what? He'd have to spend the night here in the woods, right here beneath this tree, because he had no intention of being fool enough to try to find his way back home.

It was dark. What of it? There was nothing in these woods for him to worry about—or was there? Snakes? Maybe. But they wouldn't bother him if he didn't go barging about, stepping on them. Noises? Sure there were noises. All woods had them. Birds, squirrels, insects.

He leaned against the tree trunk, hating himself for being jumpy. He tried to calm his nerves, tried to fight against an almost overpowering sensation that eyes were watching him. The feeling grew until his skin crawled.

He heard a noise, the rustling of underbrush, a

114

sniffling sound. He whirled in that direction, aimed his flashlight, and pressed the button. The feeble beam reached out and found a patch of low scrub pine. The light reflected from two eyes which looked like big white china marbles.

His breath jammed hard into his throat. He forced words out and heard his voice, high-pitched, demand, "Who's there?"

"William."

Marty swallowed hard, pulling himself together.

"William?" he repeated stupidly.

"Yes, *sir*. I'm William, all right. How're *you*, Mr. Shane?"

Relief hit Marty with a force which found its outlet in a shout of laughter. Everything seemed very funny to him now, incredible, but funny. The omnipresent William was on the job, even out here in the middle of the woods in the dead of night.

Regaining his breath, Marty finally asked, "And how do you happen to be here, William?"

"Jus' *happen* to," admitted William. "I heard voices, saw some lights, so I snuck up."

He came from behind the small tree, carrying a burlap bag which sagged beneath the weight of something in it.

"What've you got there?" Marty asked.

"Big ol' fat possum."

"Dead?"

"Oh, no, *sir*. He's alive. That's why I'm in the woods tonight. My daddy built me a trap, like a box. Catch 'em alive. Don't hurt 'em none."

"Alive?" repeated Marty, excitement creeping into his voice. "Alive, huh? Well, what do you know about that?"

"Don't know nothin'," admitted William.

"Want to sell me that possum, William?"

"No, *sir*. I *give* 'im to you."

"Thanks," said Marty. "You're a real pal, but you earned two dollars just the same." Then, as a thought struck him, he asked, "How did you get way out here?"

"Walk."

"But," said Marty in astonishment, "it must be ten or fifteen miles from town."

"No, *sir*," corrected William. " 'Tain't more'n a mile."

Marty digested this, realizing how completely he'd been hoodwinked by the Bantams. He finally said, "Well, let's get going."

He picked up the stuffed possum and followed William. The small boy moved unerringly.

"Can you see in the dark?" Marty asked.

"Yes, *sir*," admitted William. "I can see."

"Well, I'll be hanged," said Marty. Then, a little later, he said, "That possum's awful quiet. Why doesn't he kick around?"

William chuckled. "He's playin' dead. That's the way they do. Can't make 'em move 'cept by throwin' 'em in water."

Marty Shane was learning about wildlife. He considered the stuffed specimen in his own bag, and as his plans shaped up, the stuffed possum began to interfere with them. He finally decided to dispose of it when he had the chance, excusing himself with the conviction that the Bantams had had their money's worth from it. They'd had their gag. Now Marty would have his. It was too good a chance to miss, even though it might not boost his stock much with the Bantams.

Marty stopped at his own room to hide the stuffed possum, and when he reached the Bantams' clubhouse he was carrying the live one. He noted with satisfaction that Cal Steuben's car was parked in the driveway. Marty touched the radiator and found it good and hot. The hunters obviously had just returned.

Composing his features, Marty strode into the huge living room. At least twenty of the Bantams, including Marty's recent companions, were gathered there, listening with wide grins to Cal Steuben's description of the possum hunt. At Marty's entrance, Steuben choked upon his words and stared. The rest of them stared too. The silence was electric.

"Good evening, gentlemen," said Marty cheerily.

No answer.

"I brought your possum," Marty said, and proved it.

He went over to Cal Steuben's chair, opened the bag and carefully slid the possum to the floor. Steuben ogled it and gasped, "*That* ain't the one!" He leaned over as if hypnotized, touched the animal, and blurted, "It's alive!" Then repeated hoarsely, "It's alive!"

"Alive?" said Marty innocently. "Alive? Why, of course it is. Why not? I brought it back to Jake. He's been wanting one for a pet." Then worriedly, "Wasn't I *supposed* to bring it back?"

None of the Bantams had an answer, and Marty, with a nice sense of timing, gave them no chance to figure one out. He started from the room. At the door he turned and said, "Thanks, boys, for the possum hunt." And not until he reached the outside darkness did he let his grin break out.

118

# CHAPTER 11

The hunting incident, as Marty had suspected, did not endear him to the Bantams. It had finally reached the point, however, where Marty didn't care—not much, at any rate, and he cared less as the final days of intensive training passed. He was going strong, hitting solidly, and still there was no sign of a contract from Lobo Mercer.

Marty's cloak of patience, flimsy at its best, began to wear dangerously thin. He was being pushed around and knew it. His temper was fraying at the edges but he kept it under reasonable control by promising himself a final violent blowoff when all hope was gone.

The deadline came, and still no contract. The Bantams would start north the following day. It was early evening. Marty and Dinty were in their room. Both men were packing in strained silence, and Dinty kept shooting worried glances in Marty's direction. Marty's lips were stretched in a thin unpleasant smile.

Dinty finally said, "You've got me pretty worried, guy. You're cookin' up a batch of trouble."

"Do you blame me?"

"Well, no. But there's such a thing as *too* much trouble. Maybe it's none of my business, but what's on your mind?"

"I'm going to have a little chat with Mercer."

"Uh-huh. Then what?"

"Then I thought I'd drop by and visit Mugger Blain."

"Just a little friendly chitchat, huh?"

"What else? And after that I'll look up Rudy Kemp."

Dinty folded a necktie carefully, then said, "Look, Marty. I'd like to deal myself a hand in this. You've had a mighty scummy deal."

Marty straightened from his packing, stared at his roommate, and said with involuntary wonder in his voice, "Why stick *your* neck out?"

120

"Well," said Dinty, refusing in his embarrassment to meet Marty's eyes, "I just don't like to see an okay guy kicked around."

A quick warmth broke the tightness of Marty's smile. He said, "Thanks, Dinty, but it's my show. If I end up in the clink for mayhem, you can write me postcards."

Dinty shrugged. "Okay," he said. "Okay."

There was silence for a short time longer. Then Marty closed his suitcase, stretched, and said, "Well, I'll be on my way."

"Doggone it, guy, be *careful!*" Dinty blurted.

"Oh, sure," said Marty. "Sure." He started for the door.

"Well," offered Dinty gloomily. "Good luck, at any rate."

Marty found Lobo Mercer in his room. He had expected to find him there, involved in a lot of last minute desk work concerning the Bantams' departure from the training camp.

The door was open, and Marty walked in without knocking. Mercer, in his shirt sleeves, glanced up sharply from the papers strewn before him on the table. His gaze narrowed with a quick defensive look as he spotted the danger flags in Marty's eyes.

Lobo Mercer, however, was a fast thinker, and his expression of alarm was fleeting. His lips stretched promptly into a genial smile of welcome, and before Marty had the chance to fire an opening broadside, Mercer's hand darted to an official-looking document, which he extended toward Marty.

"Well, Marty," he said, "glad to see you. You're just in time—and here's your contract. Look it over, Marty. You'll find it's not a bad one."

Marty reached out automatically for the paper, unballing his fist to take it in his fingers. His fingers, he found, were slightly stiff.

"I'm sorry, Marty," Mercer rattled on, "that I've had to hold it up like this and keep you on the hot seat for so long. But I'd made a verbal agreement with a Fordham University first sacker. I'd have had to sign him if he hadn't asked permission to hook up with Albany instead. I was glad to release him so I could take you on in his place. I just got word from him today."

The explanation had a vague, fishy sort of sound to Marty, but he couldn't shrug off the fact that an actual contract with the Bantams was staring him in the face, a contract he had despaired of getting. He felt deflated like a balloon. His departing anger left a big uncertain void in him.

He said, "Uh-huh." Then to cover his confusion he began looking through the contract.

It was, as Mercer had stated, a pretty good one with regard to the salary offered, although that part didn't concern Marty much. The contract was a standard form, but Marty plowed suspiciously through the legal phrasing, looking for a catch. He couldn't find one.

Mercer interrupted. "Steve Carson lives in this house too. I'll go get him while you finish reading. He'll notarize it."

Carson was the club secretary, and when Mercer left the room to get him, Marty had the chance to pull himself together. It was easier than he'd believed it might be. A feeling of elation worked its way into his veins, causing the irritation of the previous days to fade. His uppermost thought now was that he had made the grade, the first important step, at any rate, toward proving to his brother, Bender Shane, that Marty Shane could get along in baseball without help.

He went through the brief proceedings in a daze. He signed his name, had it notarized, shook hands with Lobo Mercer, and started back for his room. He was still in a mild fog when he got there. Dinty was waiting, making no effort to conceal the fact he had been pacing up and down the floor.

"I'm in!" yelped Marty.

Dinty stood and stared at him. "You're *what?*" he demanded hoarsely.

"I'm a Bantam."

Dinty collapsed into a chair. "I don't get it," he

complained irritably. "It doesn't make sense. I thought I was a wise guy. I figured I knew all the angles, but now it looks as if I'm just a dope."

Marty's confidence was returning fast. "What puzzles you, my boy?" he grinned.

"It's a bigger chance than I figured Lobo dared to take. He's spitting in Rudy Kemp's face. If you don't make good, and fast, Rudy'll ride Lobo bald-headed. Lobo knows that, yet he signs you."

"So what?" demanded Marty, a small chip on his shoulder. "Why shouldn't I make good—and fast? I can outslug any guy on the club. Mercer needs a slugger. *That's* why he signed me."

Dinty said pointedly, "You can't field your position for sour beans. You could if you wanted to, but you won't take the trouble to learn. That's the truth, and you can get sore if you want to."

Marty thought it over, then said decisively, "No use getting sore, because you're probably right. What I say is, if a man can bat above .400 he doesn't *have* to field."

"Okay," Dinty said resignedly. Then he added plaintively, "But I *still* can't figure it out."

"Don't try," said Marty airily. "Just leave it to your Uncle Marty."

It was a statement of high faith, but some of Marty's early confidence began to ooze away next morning at the breakfast table. It was the final meal at the training camp. The Bantams were full of ginger, but made it obvious, without too much tact, that they had no wish, as yet, to share their ginger with the latest Bantam member. If they drew any satisfaction from the fact the club had annexed a new slugger, they didn't show it.

Marty therefore had to accept the fact that he was definitely on probation with the Bantams as the combined result of Kemp's literary efforts, together with the showdown Marty had failed to accept with Mugger Blain.

Facing the situation helped a little, but not much. It brought one fact into sharp, alarming focus. He'd have to make good as a first baseman pronto. If he didn't, he'd have the entire club, with the exception of Jake and Dinty, on his back.

It was not a pleasant prospect, because Marty had sense enough to understand the value of good feeling on a ball club. If the men continued to resent him, he knew it could act as a subtle poison, a poison which, through the medium of ragged nerves, would ultimately affect his batting average.

The Bantams, all except Marty, left by train shortly after breakfast. Marty flew north in his Cloudbuster, having made previous arrangements for keeping his plane at a private airport near Buffalo.

The trip was not as pleasant as he'd hoped it

would be. Instead of enjoying the relaxing solitude of the air, he kept worrying about his first appearance in a league game with the Bantams. It began to scare him just a little. He fought against the feeling without too much success, finding that his pores exuded chilly sweat at unexpected times.

# CHAPTER 12

Marty's condition of jumpy nerves had not improved on the date of the Bantams' opening game, a few days after their arrival. The curtain-raiser was against the Akron Bisons, and Marty learned through Dinty Mead that the game was a continuation of the blood feud which had existed for many years between the two teams. The Brooklyn Dodgers and the New York Giants were close pals compared to the Bantams and the Bisons. The Bisons, in fact, had stolen the flag from under the very noses of the Bantams on the previous year, and the Bantam fans were rabid in their desire to shellac the visiting Bisons in the opener. The Bantams felt like that about it, too.

Marty tried to calm his jitters with the almost certain belief that Mercer would not let him make his debut in a game of such importance. Wally Gant had recovered from the pulled muscle in his leg, and, because of his steadiness and experience, was the logical man to play first base against the Bisons. Marty assured himself of this, even though he knew that nothing was certain in the game of baseball.

He also tried to excuse the butterflies in his stomach by telling himself he wasn't *really* scared to play, but that a few days in the dugout would help him learn the ropes. It was a poor subterfuge. He was ashamed of it. He finally looked the situation right between the eyes and admitted he *was* scared. Scared of the crowd, and of the effect their reception of him might have upon his game. He wanted to postpone the thing as long as possible.

The postponement, however, was denied him. The move from south to north had given Wally Gant a bad cold. On the morning of the game, Lobo Mercer said to Marty, "I'm going to have to start you, Marty. Wally's in no shape to play. I hadn't intended to stick you in so soon, but now I've got to. It's an important game, Marty, a mighty important game. Think you can keep that first sack covered?"

Marty swallowed and said, "Sure I can," hoping

the words did not reflect the actual condition of his thoughts.

Nothing happened to improve his state of mind before the Bantams started for the field in the early afternoon. Pregame tension in the locker room was high. The Bantams wanted to salt this game away.

With one exception, none of them showed open resentment over the fact that the first sack was to be entrusted to Marty Shane. The exception was Mugger Blain, who was taking the mound for the Bantams. It was an important game for Blain because it marked his first step on the comeback trail. He needed a win, and he wanted plenty of support behind him. The glances he shot at Marty were all sour. He finally said, loud enough for Marty to hear, "It ain't bad enough that I got to worry about the batters. I got to worry about my first baseman too."

Marty jerked his head up, but kept his mouth shut and went back to his dressing. He had enough on his mind at the moment without starting something with Mugger Blain. He was taut as a fiddle string when the Bantams went out for their warm-up session.

And he soon found that the apprehension behind his tautness was not without foundation. When he parked himself in his position for fielding practice, he could feel the resentment of the fans as they gave him a critical once-over. They had all been primed by the daily written comments of Rudy Kemp. They were ready to expect the worst. In addition, they were fond of Wally Gant, and to see his position taken by an upstart was a lot for them to swallow.

One fan behind first base stood it as long as he could, then yelled, "You'd better show us somethin', Shane! We got our eyes on ya! There ain't no place for phonies on *this* club!"

It was not a comment calculated to soothe Marty's nerves. His ears turned red, and he felt an itchy place between his shoulder blades where the stares of the fans were concentrated. He tried to do a little concentrating of his own, to keep his attention riveted upon the warm-up.

It wasn't so bad at first, because he noticed, significantly, that Lobo Mercer, who usually sent fungos to the outfield, today was batting grounders to the infield, and the reason for the change was soon apparent. Mercer lined out hot skippers to the other infield spots, but the ones he sent to first were easy bounders. Marty was grateful for the break, even though he knew that Mercer's own interests were at stake.

It began to look as if Marty Shane might weather the practice session until he became involved in one of those pepper outbreaks where the infield flashes the ball around to show its accuracy and speed.

Trying to fit into the spirit of the thing and to maintain the rattling tempo, Marty uncorked a throw to third without setting himself properly for it. The ball sailed six feet over Okie Gordon's head.

It was what the fans had waited for, and they cut loose like a pack of wolves. They yapped and howled. They wanted to know what Marty Shane was doing on a good team like the Bantams—what right he had to be there. And while they were still squawking, Marty missed a low throw from the second sacker, Andy Harker.

It was a snap throw which hit the dirt in front of Marty. It should have been an easy pick-up. At the least, he should have stopped it, but by this time he was in such a dither that the ball shot between his legs like a greased pig, ending up against the boxes.

Marty would have preferred to walk up and slap a tiger on the nose rather than retrieve the ball he'd just missed. He set his jaw, though, and went after it, presenting a blank face to the withering blast of ridicule which engulfed him from the grandstand. It was hard to take, but he plowed through, picked up the ball, and threw it back.

Although the remainder of the practice session was uneventful, the damage had been done. Marty didn't kid himself. He knew he'd managed to get off to the worst start possible, and the job ahead of him loomed more formidable than ever.

131

However, the overall effect on him was beneficial. It made him sore in a steady sort of way. It also made his position clear. The fans had declared war. They were his open enemies. That part was good, because it wiped away all uncertainty, told him where he stood. It meant a fight, and the prospects of a good brawl always found Marty at his best. His nerves were still tight, it was true, but in a different way. It was the sort of tightness he could understand.

He participated grimly in the opening ceremonies, believing they would never end. A visiting congressman finally heaved out the first ball, having trouble getting it past his stomach. Cal Steuben managed to catch the toss. The umpire yelled, "Play ball!" and the game was on.

The first Bison came to the plate. Marty took his place, hands on knees. The Bantams were talking it up, making lots of noise. Marty kept his mouth shut, tight-lipped, hoping the first ball would not come in his direction.

Mugger Blain tossed the resin bag aside, toed the slab, looked the Bison over carefully, then went into his windup. He blazed the first one past the batter's knees for a called strike. The fans let out a pent-up yell, then settled back to watch the game.

The Bison lead-off man was nervous. He had a right to be because Mugger Blain was hot. He sneaked in a fast-breaking hook for the second strike. The batter chopped at it—and missed. The third pitch was a bit high, but the Bison tried for it anyway, nicking it foul into the screen. Blain served up a change of pace on the fourth ball, and the batter almost broke his back. He went down swinging. The Bantam fans let out an approving bellow.

The second Bison got a small chunk of the first pitch. The ball looped behind the plate in a towering foul. Cal Steuben yanked his mask off, spotted the ball, and went back after it. He made a nice catch near the screen for the second out.

The third Bison waited out two balls, took a called strike, then connected sloppily with the fourth pitch. It was a slow bouncing grounder down to short, the sort of exaggerated bunt which a fast runner can sometimes turn into a fluke hit.

Dinty Mead came in on the ball like a whippet. Marty leaped for the bag, his heart jamming in his throat at the sudden prospect of his first put-out in pro baseball. The play would be close, mighty close, and Marty found time for a panicky prayer that Dinty's peg would be a good one. The runner was coming fast.

Dinty didn't have much time. He made the pickup on a dead sprint, and snapped an underhand throw while still bent halfway to the ground. Marty tensed himself for almost anything, but it was wasted apprehension. The peg came in like a bullet to a bull's-eye, chest high, dead center. Marty couldn't have missed it if he'd tried, and the runner was out by half a stride. The fans gave Dinty a big hand, but didn't overlook Marty Shane. A leather-lunged fan yelled, "Great catch, Shane! Great catch! We didn't think ya had it in ya. What a fielder! What a fielder!"

Catching the spirit of the thing, more fans joined in with loud sarcastic comment. Marty felt like throwing the ball right into the middle of them, but he kept his head, tossed it to Blain, and started with the other Bantams toward the dugout. His muscles were twitching in a way he didn't like. The fans had burrowed their way beneath his hide again.

Dinty Mead was lead-off man for the Bantams. As he went to the plate he got a hand for the fast play he'd made in the first half of the inning. He pulled the cap visor lower on his eyes and faced Fog Streeter, the Bisons' big right-hander.

Streeter was on his way up, climbing fast, im-proving every time he pitched. The Tigers, it was rumored, had him all tied up, and would probably call on him this season. The kid was good.

His first offering to Dinty gave an inkling of what he had in the way of speed. The ball came through in a blurred streak, cutting the center of the pan and crashing hard into the catcher's mitt. Dinty merely stared at it, then hunched his shoulders and took a firmer toe hold in the dirt.

Streeter's next pitch was a hook. It broke like a boomerang, but Dinty had it spotted. He let it go as it failed to cut a corner of the plate. The count was one and one. Streeter sent in another bender on the third pitch, but it was a little close and Dinty let that one go by too. Two and one.

The fourth toss was meant to be a teaser, a change of pace with a lazy hook tacked on the tail. Dinty, however, refused to be teased. He slashed through with a compact swing, and lined a whistling grounder between third and short. It was a clean single, landing Dinty Mead on first.

From his coaching box at first, Lobo Mercer signed Swede Hansen to lay down a bunt. Hansen went for the first ball pitched and nudged it down the third base line. It was a pretty husky nudge, however, and the third baseman, coming in fast, scooped it up and figured he had a chance to make the force at second. He made his try, a nice peg, but underestimated Dinty's speed. Dinty hooked into the bag, safe by a whisker, and Hansen reached first on a fielder's choice.

Things looked pretty bright for the Bantams about then, but the good news didn't last when Kip Jurgen, center fielder, banged a grounder to the Bison second baseman, who, with the aid of the shortstop, pulled off a double play. Dinty got to third. Two men were down, and Marty Shane, cleanup man, went toward the plate.

The Bantam fans, making no bones about it, told Marty what they wanted. They wanted a hit to score a run. They wanted early proof that Marty Shane was as formidable with a war club as he was supposed to be. Now was his chance to do his stuff, and the rooters made it plain.

It was a nasty spot, but Marty accepted it with narrowed eyes and steady hands. He liked tough going, and this unquestionably was it. This was his department of the game, the hitting end. He faced Fog Streeter calmly.

Streeter tried him with a low hook. Marty let it pass for a ball. A fireball came in next. It shot sparks all the way. It was, in fact, a whole lot faster than Marty was prepared for. He swung late, getting only a small piece of it for a dribbling ground foul behind first base. He made a mental note to make allowance for Fog Streeter's speed.

The third pitch was a hook, a fast one. Marty was waiting for a hook. As the ball broke away from him, and down, he swung. His wrists were stiffened to absorb the shock, but no shock came. Once more he'd underestimated Streeter. Marty carved a big hole in the air, but that was all. The pitcher was ahead, one–two.

Marty didn't let it worry him. He still had one strike left, and he always figured it was all he needed. He was learning things he had to know about Fog Streeter. The man was good. So what?

Streeter tried him with another curve, but Marty had his eye on it. He let it pass, and the umpire called a ball. The count was even. Streeter shook off the catcher's signal, then got one that satisfied him.

It was a change of pace which almost caught Marty napping. His swing was early. He had to make a forward lunge to reach the ball at all, and barely managed a slow foul behind third. It was another lesson learned. He had a line on Fog Streeter's slow ball now.

On the sixth pitch Streeter tried to make him bite on one inside and low. Marty passed it up, and the count was full. It was a ticklish moment, but the pitcher was in as big a hole as Marty—in fact, bigger.

They studied each other intently. The guessing game was on. The advantage, however, was still with Marty, because the Bison battery had no line on his batting strengths or weaknesses. Even the outfield didn't know where to play him, so they played him deep and straight away.

Marty decided to let Streeter and his catcher do all the guessing, and to be prepared for anything they might dish up. Marty wanted a hit, of course, but he wouldn't turn his nose up at a free pass.

Streeter took his stretch, checked the man at third, then launched the payoff ball.

It wasn't a fireball. Therefore, Marty reasoned instantly, it would be a hook. It was pointed toward the outside corner of the plate, which meant that when the ball began to bend it would miss the plate entirely for a certain ball.

Marty was so sure of this, in fact, that he left his bat upon his shoulder. The bat was still upon his shoulder when the ball plunked solidly into the catcher's mitt. And not until the sound struck heavily against his ears did Marty realize that the pitch had scarcely bent at all. It had nipped the corner of the plate, and that's the way the umpire called it.

Marty Shane was out. He'd missed his chance to bring Dinty home. He had stood there like a moron, not even trying for the final pitch that any high school kid might easily have walloped. The shock left Marty numb, incredulous. Then the Bantam fans went to work on him, and really did a job.

They were still at it when he took the field again. Even his teammates eyed him with a new distaste. He tried to build a shell around himself, but he couldn't build one thick enough. He was hoping desperately no batted balls would come at him until he'd had a chance to pull himself together—if he could.

It was Mugger Blain who handed him that chance, and Marty Shane was grateful for it, even though it came from Blain. The Bantam hurler settled down to show the local yokels what real pitching was. He was cool, deliberate, and deadly. Even Marty was forced to the admission.

Marty had only one more fielding chance in the first three innings, an assist from Harker, but the peg was good and Marty hung on to it. He was getting a grip on himself now, feeling better.

Streeter, the Bison moundster, was also hot but not exactly sizzling. He kept out of trouble until the bottom of the third when the top of the Bantam list came up again. Dinty Mead went out on a looping fly to short right, but Swede Hansen banged out a single over second.

Kip Jurgen connected with a hard grounder to the first baseman who knocked it down but didn't recover it in time to make the play at second. He flipped it to Streeter, who had covered first, and got it there in time to retire Jurgen by a stride.

With two down and Hansen in scoring position on second, Marty Shane came to the plate again. The setup was similar to that of the first inning. A hit would score a run. Marty had his chance again, but was greeted by discouraged groans from the Bantam fans.

The batter's box as usual, though, had its soothing effect on Marty Shane. The mere act of stepping inside the narrow white-lined rectangle was like moving into a small world of his own where the borders were insulated against sound. He forgot the crowd. He turned his thoughts on Streeter, remembering the things he'd learned in his first trip to the plate.

Streeter uncorked his dazzling speed on the first pitch. He tried to cut the corner of the plate, outside and just above the knees. He was successful.

So was Marty. It was a clean hit and the ball howled over the shortstop's head with twenty feet to spare, reaching the left field wall before a Bison laid a hand on it. Marty went into second standing up, while Hansen loafed across the plate.

The Bantam fans let out an involuntary yell before they realized what they'd done. Then chagrin swept over them as they relapsed into the guilty silence of a kid caught stealing cookies. They didn't want to be grateful to Marty Shane, but Marty had put them on the spot. He grinned to himself, feeling better than he'd felt for days. Let the beefers chew on *that* two-bagger for a while. He was tempted to thumb his nose at them, but restrained the urge.

# CHAPTER 13

Marty expired on second because Joe Peel popped out on an infield fly. Marty started for the dugout to get his mitt, and as he passed the Bantams who were heading for the field he tried to keep his face impassive.

Dinty yelped, "Nice bingle, keed!"

A few of the others attempted belated offerings of commendation, but their hearts weren't in it. They couldn't overcome completely their previous restraint toward Marty, even though the timely hit he'd just presented them was nothing to be taken lightly.

Nevertheless, Marty recognized it as a definite step in the right direction, both with the Bantams and with the fans. The latter were pointedly silent as to wisecracks, and Marty had an unconfirmed but persistent feeling he was closer to the Bantams than he'd been all season. He'd put them in the lead in this important game, which was something they couldn't very well forget.

Mugger Blain should have been the one to feel most grateful, but if he felt that way he didn't show it. His glances toward first were as impersonal as ever. Just the same, he settled down to pitch as if the single run was all he needed.

He had the Bisons eating out of his hand for the next three innings. The Bantams collected three scattered hits in the fourth and fifth innings, but Streeter kept his head, worked hard, and stayed out of trouble.

Marty came to the plate again in the bottom of the sixth. He stepped up as the lead-off man, and was quick to sense a different attitude in the Bantam fans. They didn't yell encouragement, it was true, but there was a compromise to their silence which told Marty they were at least willing to be shown.

He waited out a pair of balls, then tied into the third pitch. He caught a low hook on the end of his bat and bashed it into right field for a single. The fans liked it, and were fair enough to tell him so. Perched on the first sack, Marty Shane felt pretty good.

Peel tried to sacrifice him down to second, but made a feeble job of it. His bunt popped high into the air, and Streeter didn't have to leave his tracks to pull it in. Streeter tried to catch Marty off first base, but Marty was too fast for him. He got back in time.

Cal Steuben got a nice chunk of the first pitch for a wallop over second, but the center fielder came in fast and took it off his shoestrings for the second out. Then Mercer reached into his bag of tricks. He signed Marty to try for second on the first pitch.

It was a sound tactical maneuver, because Marty's long legs possessed a speed the Bisons had no reason to suspect. Marty took a modest lead then exploded into action at Streeter's first business gesture toward the batter.

It was a beautiful piece of larceny. Marty stretched along the path like a greyhound after a mechanical rabbit. He saw the second baseman reaching for the throw, but the guy was reaching high. Marty hit the dirt and went into the bag in a cloud of dust, safe by a city block.

The fans cut loose again. This time there was some honest gusto in their roar. They were beginning to like this rookie, Marty Shane, whether they wanted to or not. They couldn't hold out on a guy who delivered hits and stolen bases.

And then, to make the picture perfect, Okie Gordon smacked a liner over the third baseman's head. Marty was away with the crack of the bat, his long legs driving hard. Wally Gant, coaching at third, waved him home, but yelled as Marty rounded the bag, "It'll be close, Marty! Hit the dirt!"

It *was* close. The left fielder came in fast and made a wicked peg. Marty streaked into his slide. He closed his eyes against the spouting dust. He heard the ball smack in the catcher's mitt, then felt the catcher fall upon him.

Marty was scared he hadn't made it, but his doubts were soon cleared up. The thunder from the Bantam fans was all he had to hear. They wouldn't have yelled like that if the umpire had jerked his thumb into the air. The score was 2–0, with the Bantams on the right end of the count.

Okie Gordon went to second on the throw-in, but he got no farther. Streeter bore down hard on Harker and struck him out to retire the side. When Marty took his fielding spot at first, there was a tentative ripple of applause. Not much, but enough to show the temperature was rising.

Mugger Blain got into trouble in the top of the seventh. In fact, quite a lot of trouble. The first Bison rapped a single over short. Blain walked the second man, and when the umpire called the fourth ball Blain howled as if he'd been stabbed. He started for the umpire, but Lobo Mercer reached Blain first and sent him back to the mound, red-necked.

Blain grooved his first pitch to the third batter and the Bison climbed all over it for a homer into the right field bleachers. Three runs came in. The Bantam fans were shocked and wordless. A pall of gloom hung over them. A pair of Bantam relief hurlers started warming up hurriedly in the bull pen.

Mercer didn't have to use them, though, because Mugger Blain did not blow up. He had courage. Even Marty Shane was forced to concede it. Blain struck out the next three men to face him.

Nevertheless, the Bantams were trailing by one run, a situation which was not remedied in the seventh or eighth innings. The score was still 3–2 at the top of the ninth, and the Bantams were under a terrific tension.

Nor was the tension eased when the lead-off Bison clipped a single to right field. The second man went out on a high foul to Okie Gordon. The third man at the plate topped a dribbling grounder to Mugger Blain. Blain fielded it, whirled, and tried for the force at second. His throw was a whisker late. So was the play at first. Both men were safe. One out.

145

The fourth Bison lined a sizzling grounder down to short. Dinty fielded it with his usual coordinated speed, and flipped a toss to second for the force-out. Andy Harker spun about and made his peg to first. It wasn't good. It was in the dirt. A top-flight fielder would have nabbed it. Marty didn't. He merely blocked it in time to hold the man on third.

Blain started for first base, his expression ugly. Mercer, from the coaching box, snapped, "Easy, Mugger!"

Blain swallowed hard and pulled himself together. Marty tossed the ball to him, and Blain went back to the mound. Because of Marty's error, there was still one Bison to retire.

Blain retired him, but not unassisted. The batter poled a line drive between short and second. It would have gone for a certain hit except for the miraculous fielding of Dinty Mead. He dove through the air and speared it with his glove. He hit the dirt, rolled over once, but came up with the ball snugly in his mitt.

When the Bisons took the field for the bottom half of the ninth, Mugger Blain started for the bat pile to take his turn at the plate, but Mercer stopped him. A pinch hitter. Art Taylor would go in for Blain. Blain came to the dugout, his blood pressure still dangerously high. The other men, taking their places on the bench, shot worried looks at him.

The big pitcher was in a nasty mood, and the Bantams knew it. Mercer was outside talking to Taylor. Blain, low-voiced, cut loose on Marty Shane.

"You lousy excuse for a first bagger! What're you tryin' to do? Toss the game for me?"

Marty pulled in a long slow breath of satisfaction. This wasn't exactly the moment he had waited for, the setup was not quite right, but it would do until a better one came along. And as he savored the moment in his mind he framed it to the best of his ability.

"You're a sorehead, Blain," he said in even tones. "A loud-mouthed, noisy sorehead. I'm going to bat your ears down, Blain. I'm going to change that ugly pan of yours. I'm going to work on you as soon as this game's over. I'll see you in the locker room. We'll stall till Lobo leaves, then have it out. Is it a date?"

Blain's jaw dropped open. Most of the Bantams' jaws, in fact, dropped open. Neither Blain nor the Bantams had anticipated this from Marty Shane. Blain's teeth clicked shut. He said with relish, "It's a date."

Marty nodded briefly, then turned his attention to the game. He could feel the glances which the other Bantams shot in his direction. He could feel a new and different quality in their attitudes toward him. They liked the way he'd talked to Blain. The seed of respect was sprouting in their minds. Their attention, by degrees, refocused on the diamond.

Taylor came through with a hit. He laid a surprise bunt down the third base line and set out for first like a scalded cat. He beat the throw by a fraction of a stride. Sensing a late rally, the Bantam fans began to yell.

Dinty Mead increased the volume of their yelling. He clouted a lusty single over third, but the left fielder handled it in time to hold Taylor on second.

Swede Hansen tied into the third pitch for a long low fly, but the right fielder pulled it down near the foul line after a spectacular running catch. With one out, young Streeter took a hitch in his breeches and sent Kip Jurgen down swinging.

And thus the stage was set again for Marty Shane. He couldn't have found a more dramatic moment in a movie script. He knew what was ahead of him, understood its vast importance, but he didn't let it shake him—not with his feet once firmly planted in the batter's box. The familiar feeling of complete steadiness came over him. It was almost like being hypnotized, like being in a small tight world which excluded everybody but the pitcher and himself.

Streeter was nervous, as he had a right to be. He had done a fine courageous job, but the job was not quite finished. He still had Marty Shane to polish off, and he knew now that Shane was dangerous. Fog Streeter had to pitch with care.

The first offering was wide, outside. It threw a quick scare into Marty. Maybe they were going to pass him. But common sense refuted this. With Bantams on first and second the Bisons already had the setup for a double play. Furthermore, Joe Peel, who followed Marty on the batting list, was always a dangerous man, a veteran, deadly in the clutches.

Marty's reasoning proved sound. The next ball was low, inside, but not intentionally that way. Streeter was merely trying to keep his offerings where Marty couldn't hit them easily.

Marty let the third pitch pass him too, a hook which broke too soon and went for the third ball. Marty glanced toward Mercer in the first base coaching box for the take or hit sign. Marty's heart took a grateful bounce. Mercer had signed "Hit."

Fog Streeter sent the cripple down the slot. It came in fast and smoky, just the way Marty liked them. He swung from his toes, putting everything he had into the clout. He felt the solid shock up through his wrists and arms. He started for first base, but cut his speed before he reached the bag. No need to hurry now. The ball was already in the pocket of a bleacher fan. Taylor and Mead loped in ahead of him. The baseball game was over.

There was no longer doubt as to the Bantam fans'

opinion of the rookie, Marty Shane. They were crazy about him. For the moment, anyway, he was the fair-haired boy. He'd come through with a roaring homer when the chips were down, and a fan could ask for nothing more than that.

Neither could Marty Shane. He was pleased with himself, justly pleased. The Bantams in their first exuberance piled all over him, a demonstration which made him feel no worse.

He had a puzzled moment, though, when a quick reserve became apparent in the Bantams. Their first impulsiveness eased off. They began to look at him a trifle strangely.

Then suddenly he knew what it was all about. The brightness of the moment had caused him to forget. He had a date with Mugger Blain, a date to knock the stuffing out of Blain—assuming that he could.

The wide grin left his face. A tight smile took its place. Slow anger found its way once more into his veins. He had had his big moment in the batter's box, and now he was about to have another in the locker room—if everything went well, if Mercer left in time.

# CHAPTER 14

The atmosphere of the locker room was filled with static. The natural jubilation of a winning club predominated, but underneath the jubilation was the taut anticipation of excitement yet to come.

Lobo Mercer must have sensed it the moment he stepped into the room. He reminded Marty of a hunting dog whose nose had just discovered a covey of quail. The manager pulled up short, let the feeling creep into his bones, then moved his eyes slowly around the room.

"What goes on here?" he demanded shortly.

No one saw fit to answer, so Mercer called upon his instinct. His gaze came to rest on Mugger Blain, shifted suddenly to Marty, then back to Blain. Mercer nodded imperceptibly as if satisfied with his deduction.

"So that's it, huh?" he said as if talking to himself. Then, pointedly, to Blain, "Okay, let's have it, Mugger. Speak up."

Blain didn't try to stall. He said, "Shane promised to bat my ears down. I'm waiting for him to begin."

Turning to Marty, Mercer asked, "How about it, Marty?"

"That's what I promised him," admitted Marty. "And that's what he's going to get—now or later. He bawled me out back in the training camp, and got away with it. He bawled me out again today, and he's *not* getting away with it."

"Don't you think that's something for *me* to decide?" demanded Mercer.

"Yes," admitted Marty frankly, "I do. But the catch is, Lobo, that it's bound to happen sooner or later anyway, and it's better for it to happen here than sometime during a game. I'd like to promise you to behave myself, but I'm sure I'd break the promise if Blain ever pops off at me again."

"Have you considered the fact," said Mercer

bluntly, "that I might kick you off the squad?"

"Yes," said Marty calmly. "I've considered it."

"How about you, Mugger?" Mercer asked.

"Shane put it about right," Blain conceded sullenly. "I don't like to have an infield jugglin' the ball behind me, and Shane'll keep on jugglin' it. When he does, I'll tell 'im what I think."

"Even if I kick you off the club?" asked Mercer.

"Sorry, Lobo," Blain replied. "But that's the way I'm built. I want to get my hands on him. Maybe it makes me sound like a mug, but I can't help that either. Shane *did* win my game for me today. I got to give him credit for it. He can bat. But in other ways I think the bum's a phony."

Mercer thought it over, weighing the elements with care. He pondered at such length that the Bantams were shifting restlessly. The movement of their cleats made grating noises on the floor. Marty was wound up tight inside. He was all set for a showdown, and he didn't want it postponed indefinitely by any compromise Mercer might think up. An involuntary grunt of satisfaction came from him when Mercer said, "Okay, boys. You can fight it out."

There was a gusty sound in the locker room as the Bantams all released their breath. There was a general movement toward the sides of the room as the men left ample space for fighting in the middle. Mercer, however, brought a quick end to their anticipation.

"Relax," he said abruptly. "We're not holding the fight here. What sort of a chump do you think I am? Do you think I'd take the chance that one of the fools would fall against a steel locker or a bench? They're too valuable—even if they haven't got any brains."

There were mutterings of disappointment, which Mercer interrupted promptly.

"We'll do this thing up right. We'll make a real bout of it, with gloves that'll be heavy enough to cut down the risk of a busted hand. We'll stage the bout in Terry's Gym. Terry's a friend of mine, and he'll let us use the ring for a little while tomorrow morning. Mugger won't have to pitch again for several days, and I intended to use Wally Gant at first tomorrow anyway. So that's the setup. Tomorrow, ten o'clock at Terry's Gym. No admission. We'll keep it a closed affair. Nobody permitted but the Bantams. Does that suit everybody?"

Evidently it did. It also suited Marty Shane, because common sense told him he'd have a better chance against Blain with boxing rules in force. Blain would be a mighty dangerous man in a bare-knuckled brawl. The arrangements seemed to suit Blain too. He was grinning tightly as he shed his clothes.

*　　*　　*

Marty started for the gym next morning with his two friends, Dinty and Jake.

"How do you feel?" asked Dinty anxiously.

"Fine," said Marty truthfully.

"Don't underestimate him," Dinty warned.

"I'm trying not to," Marty said. "I'm even conceding he might lick me, but if he does he'll know he's been in a battle. It's a funny thing," he went on thoughtfully, "but all I seem to want is to feel his hide beneath my fists. I don't seem to care too much how it comes out, just so I can clout him a few times with everything I've got. If I can do *that*, I'll work a lot of poison out of my system."

Dinty nodded. "I know how you feel," he said.

Most of the Bantams were at Terry's Gym when Marty got there. A few late-comers barged in worriedly as if afraid of missing something. There was a hum of high excitement in the air. The Bantams stared at Marty when he entered, but Marty scarcely noticed them. He was concentrating on the fight.

Terry, an old pug with scrambled ears, took Marty in charge, led him to a dressing room and fitted him with boxing shoes and shorts. Terry also taped his hands with expert speed. It was a snug professional job. He told Marty that Mugger Blain was in another dressing room, ready to go.

155

Blain was in the gym when Marty came outside. Blain was bouncing about, shadow-boxing, warming up. Marty followed suit, feeling silly, but he realized the stupidity of stepping into the ring cold.

Terry finally asked in a businesslike way, "You guys ready?"

Marty said,"Yes." Blain nodded.

Terry went on. "I'm refereein' the bout. It'll go six three-minute rounds to a decision—if it lasts that long. I'm givin' you boys each a good second, but he won't give you no advice. You'll be on your own. Okay, climb into the ring."

The two men straddled through the ropes and went to their stools in opposite corners. Terry produced two pairs of new gloves.

Seeing the shiny red mitts, Blain snorted, "What! Those pillows?"

They were ten-ounce gloves, regulation size for amateur heavyweights. Blain wanted lighter ones. Marty also would have preferred gloves with less padding, but he kept his mouth shut.

While the gloves were being laced upon his hands, Marty let his eyes move across to Blain. It wasn't a reassuring sight. Blain's muscles were laid in artistic ropes along his arms and shoulders. His chest was deep. He was heavier than Marty. Marty thrust the disturbing thoughts aside, then drew his mind into a shell of concentration. He hoped his boxing skill was not too rusty. On the other hand, Blain's was bound to be rusty too.

When the gloves were tied, Terry called the two men to the center of the ring, gave them a short lecture on the rules, then sent them back to their corners. The stools had been removed. The time-keeper, one of Terry's men, had his eyes on the watch, his hand upon the bell. His hand moved. The bell rang. The fight was on.

Marty slid toward the center of the ring. Blain came out, his guard up, moving smoothly with all the earmarks of a pro. There was no indecision in his eyes or motions. There was something formi-dable about him, more formidable than Marty Shane had ever found in any previous opponent.

Marty's nerves began to jump. It worried him. He circled cautiously to the left, trying to give his nerves a chance to settle down as Blain moved in.

Blain must have sensed Marty's early apprehen-sion. Blain flicked an experimental left for Marty's head. Marty's breath hissed sharply through his teeth, and he hated himself for permitting Blain to see his nervousness.

Marty pawed at the jab with his right hand, but failed to brush it off. It landed lightly. Marty scarcely felt it—but he felt the next blow, a crashing right hook to his body.

It hit the lowered elbow of his left arm. Otherwise Marty would have been in serious trouble. He didn't know how his elbow happened to be down there. Probably luck, but it served its purpose. The wallop jolted his wind, but not too seriously. Marty tied Blain in a clinch, and was breathing easily again when he obeyed Terry's order to "break clean!"

Blain stepped back too, but came in fast again, trying to nail Marty before he had recovered from the hook. Marty met him with a left, a sizzling jab. It went in with a speed Blain couldn't block. It smacked Blain hard upon the cheek, throwing him off balance and spoiling the aim of another right hook to the ribs. The glove whizzed past Marty's washboard belly. He shot a right at Blain's exposed head, and there was enough steam behind it to draw Blain into a clinch.

But Blain broke the clinch himself before Terry had a chance to order it. Blain thrust Marty backward with a sweep of his powerful arms.

But Marty caught his balance swiftly. His footwork always had been sound. He expected Blain to come charging in again, but Blain took time to think it over. He was probably pondering that left jab of Marty's, wondering if it had been a fluke or if Marty really was that good.

Blain made his decision swiftly, deciding probably that the jab had been a lucky stab. There was a hungry, impatient glitter in Blain's eyes. His con-

fidence in himself was still supreme, and he wanted
to polish off Marty Shane as swiftly as he'd promised to.

So he jumped to the attack again, once more
without the proper caution. He found it out when
Marty proved his left jab was no phony. He zinged
it in again to nail Blain solidly upon the forehead.
Blain's head snapped back, but he kept on coming.
He looped a hard left at Marty's head, but Marty
caught most of the force upon his shoulder. Blain
banged another right at Marty's belly, and Marty
stopped it with his arm.

Blain kept on slugging, barging in, trying to drop
Marty with sheer weight of armament. It didn't
work, because Marty kept his feet. He took a lot
of punishment but nothing serious, a fact which
might have warned Blain if he hadn't been so eager
for a knockout.

Marty gave ground, keeping well covered up. He
refused to clinch because something important was
taking place inside him. The mauling was actually
quieting his nerves, making him forget his jitters.
Violent action of this sort was what he'd needed.

The doggedness of Blain's attack kept Marty's
arms busy with defense. He didn't have a chance
to haul a fist back for a counterblow, but his
thoughts were clicking accurately as he waited for
an opening.

He got it when Blain forced him to the ropes. Blain drew his arm back for a slugging left, leaving his jaw exposed. Marty's right fist traveled upward. It was a short, sharp blow and he had his legs and weight behind it. It cracked against Blain's chin with jolting force.

Blain's eyes glazed momentarily; then his boxing instinct took command. His arms drew Marty in a clinch before he could slide clear along the ropes. Blain hung on cagily until the referee had forced his way between them. When Blain stepped back his eyes were clear and shrewdly calculating.

He was weighing what he'd learned, giving it swift consideration. The interim was brief, two seconds at the most, but Marty had the feeling he could read Blain's thoughts.

Blain had tumbled finally to the fact that Marty was no setup, that Marty had some ring experience of his own. The speed of Marty's left jab was a giveaway. It was the most important blow in boxing, and Marty Shane had mastered it. And the short right uppercut. No one could uncork a numbing punch in such a short distance without knowing how.

Blain was more cautious after that, and Marty took full warning from it. Now that Blain had pegged him as a formidable opponent, Blain would call upon his own skill rather than his strength.

Blain demonstrated this for the remainder of the round. He went about the deliberate business of finding out what Marty knew about the boxing game, but Marty showed him no more than he had to.

Marty also took this opportunity to learn. He studied Blain carefully as they felt each other out, and Marty found out several things which, for his own good, he tried not to accept too conclusively.

Blain's ring style was more technically sound than Marty's, but Marty became certain he himself possessed the greater speed, particularly in footwork. He could change position and recover balance faster than Mugger Blain. The relative hitting power of the two men still hung in the balance, but Marty knew it wouldn't hang there long. They were still sparring at long range when the bell went off to end the round.

Back on his stool Marty found he was breathing harder than his exertion in the first round warranted. He took quick stock of this and found the answer. He'd been holding his breath at intervals during the first round, like a novice, instead of expelling it sharply at each punch. It was something he could easily correct next round. The buzzer sounded. His second left the ring. Then the bell, and Marty moved toward the center of the canvas.

# CHAPTER 15

The second round, from the standpoint of the watchers, was a pretty dull affair. Mugger Blain still played it cagey, giving himself more time to study Marty's style, probing for a weakness. He probably believed himself to be more adept at figuring things out than Marty. Well, maybe he was, but Marty took full advantage of Blain's tactics by doing a little probing of his own. Marty was also glad for the chance to get his breathing straightened out. He worked on it with satisfactory results.

There were several flurries of fast action, without much damage done. Marty stopped a jolting left with his nose, but in return he landed a solid hook above Blain's belt, and found, to his surprise, that Blain's midsection was a little softer than it looked. Blain grunted loudly when the blow sank home. Marty fixed the item in his memory. It was an important thing to know.

He also noted something else. Blain kept his right cocked as a constant threat, but not once did he shoot it at Marty's head. Marty deliberately gave him a few small openings, and when Blain refused them Marty began to wonder why. Blain shot his left freely at Marty's head, but used his right exclusively for body punches. Not until Marty was resting between rounds did the answer come to him. It was so logical and simple he was ashamed he hadn't figured it out sooner.

Mugger Blain was saving his pitching hand, taking no chances with it. Maybe he'd had a previous injury there. Maybe he had glass knuckles which couldn't be risked in hard contact with an opponent's skull. Could be. But Marty decided not to take too much for granted.

Blain came out in the third round with the air of a man who'd solved a knotty problem and was pleased with the solution. He had apparently decided that, even though Marty might be able to match him in boxing skill, he could *not* match him in strength and weight and reach. Once more Blain showed the urge to wind the fight up fast. He came from his corner swiftly, and began to force the fighting.

Marty was smart enough to give ground, to use his speed for what he lacked in weight. He peppered at Blain with darting lefts. Most of the jabs landed. They kept Blain from getting set for a lethal punch, but they didn't stop him. He barged right through them, swinging his big fists at any target Marty offered.

Marty tried not to offer too many, but several of Blain's blows got through. They hurt. Blotches began to show on Marty's body. A lump formed on his jaw. He was landing counterblows, but most of them lacked steam. Blain gave him no chance to set himself, kept barging in, kept Marty constantly on the defensive.

Blain was making him look bad and Marty knew it. He also knew he'd have to change his tactics. He'd have to forget Blain's weight and reach and strength. He'd have to slow the big guy down. Blain had not, as yet, felt the full weight of Marty's punch, and it was time he did—past time, in fact.

So Marty watched his chance, noting critically that Blain was still using his right hand only for body punches. He was saving it for pitching, believing he wouldn't need it in this fight. Marty was certain of it now.

He based his strategy on this conviction. He weathered a barrage of heavy blows, deliberately tempting Blain to throw everything he had, forcing him to set a pace he couldn't hold, knowing Blain would have to slow down shortly for a breathing spell.

It worked out in that way. Blain checked his rush and tried to grab a few long breaths. It was the moment Marty Shane had waited for. He stopped retreating and went in at Blain, hoping to take him by surprise.

He hoped, too, that Blain would be expecting a straight left to the head, Marty's most effective blow to date. But Marty didn't shoot it this time. Instead, he dropped his left shoulder for a thundering hook to Blain's midsection. It was a good idea if it worked.

It didn't work.

The hook was on its way, too late to stop, when Marty sensed the disastrous error he had made. The instant was fleeting, an infinitesimal space of time, yet Marty's thoughts took form within the period.

He saw Blain start his right for a vicious counterpunch to Marty's head, and Marty knew he'd been outguessed, had fallen into a deadly trap. Blain was not scared, after all, of using his right hand for a Sunday punch. He had merely waited patiently, lulled Marty into carelessness. Blain had formed the whole fight toward this moment, and now his right came blasting through.

Marty had no chance to block the punch, but in the flash of time permitted him he tightened the muscles of his neck and managed to get his exposed jaw down near his shoulder.

Blain's wallop therefore landed high, but crashed against his skull with brutal force. Marty went down, hit the canvas hard upon his side. His thoughts were addled, but not paralyzed. He lay there for a moment, utterly amazed that he was conscious. He shook his head. His brain cleared swiftly. He rolled upon his stomach, then pushed himself upward in a crouch, accepting the incredible fact that his muscles still coordinated nicely. He even had sense enough to rest upon one knee while the referee counted over him. He could have stood up at the count of five, but he waited while his strength flowed back. Blain waited tautly in a neutral corner.

Marty came to his feet at the count of nine. His legs were steady as they took his weight. Blain rushed at him and threw another savage right. But this time Marty saw it coming. He didn't try to block it, just ducked under it, and braced his legs in a half crouch.

The force of Blain's momentum carried him solidly into Marty's shoulder. Marty, however, was braced to absorb the impact. He was also braced for the terrific blow he sent above Blain's waistline. It landed with a loud report. Blain grunted painfully. He tried to clinch, but Marty got in another wicked belly blow before Blain tied him up. The bell rang before the referee had a chance to separate them.

Marty relaxed in his corner and gained strength. He studied the man across from him and watched the heaving of Blain's chest as he fought hard for breath. He was breathing easier at the bell, but he looked a little worried. He came slowly from his corner, as if trying to kill time.

But Marty had no intention of permitting Blain to stall. Marty went in smoothly but with caution, respecting Blain's hitting power as well as his ring strategy.

Marty shot an experimental left. It landed, but caught Blain retreating. Marty came in steadily and Blain kept moving back, saving himself in every way he could. He let Marty do the fighting while he rested, sound tactics at this time. If Blain could weather this round without absorbing too much punishment or expending too much energy, he would be doubly dangerous in the round that followed.

So Marty knew he had to gamble. He dared not

let Blain regain his strength and wind. At the moment he was outboxing Blain, and Blain seemed satisfied to let it go at that. Yet Marty knew that Blain would not refuse a good old-fashioned slugging match—not even at this moment. If Marty met him toe to toe, Blain would accept the challenge, counting on his strength and hitting power. He might get away with it. It was the gamble Marty had to make.

He made it promptly. He plowed directly into Blain's defense, shooting rights and lefts. It was the first time Marty had shown willingness to fight like this, and Blain looked pleased. He stopped retreating and went to work.

He caught Marty with a looping left hook to the head. Marty soaked it up, and lashed a stinging right against Blain's nose. Marty grunted from a wallop to the ribs, but slashed another crashing hook into Blain's midriff.

The lid was off. The air was full of flying leather. The gym resounded to the steady smash of blows. This was the payoff, the moment each man had been waiting for. A savage pleasure flowed through Marty's veins. Blain seemed to like it too.

All science was forgotten. It was a gutter brawl. The only thing that counted now was primitive brute force, the strength to hit, to keep on hitting while the strength remained.

It couldn't last—not long, at any rate. Marty went down from another roundhouse to the head. It was a high blow, not conclusive. Marty took a count of five, then scrambled up. It was a stupid thing to do, but he had to get back in the fight.

He moved in toe to toe again with Blain. He soaked up punishment, then found a target for his right. It slammed against Blain's ear. Blain spun halfway around and hit the floor. He stayed down only briefly, heaved erect, and came back to the battle.

He was breathing heavily, sucking desperately for wind. But his nerve was sound, and he stayed right in there slugging. Marty was also fighting hard for breath, but he was in better shape than Blain. This finally dawned on him, found its way into the furious turmoil of his mind.

It also came to him that Blain was hitting with less power. He was throwing everything he had, but the wallops lacked their previous numbing force.

Up to this point, Marty had been hammering at Blain's head, forgetting the more vulnerable spots below. But now the harshness of Blain's breathing brought them back to Marty's mind.

He moved his blows lower. He sank a pair of blasting hooks, left, right, into Blain's belly. A gush of air exploded from Blain's lungs. He tried to keep his arms up, but he lacked the strength. They dropped and dangled at his sides. He stood there, glassy-eyed and helpless.

Marty could have dropped him then, but didn't. He cocked a kayo punch, then held it. Blain fought desperately to bring his arms up, then his legs gave way. He dropped upon his hands and knees and struggled hard for air. The referee began to count. Blain made several spasmodic efforts to regain his feet, and failed. The fight was over.

Marty wobbled to his corner and sat down. He was battered, bruised, and weary. He was also utterly confused. Where, he wondered, was the elation he'd been sure he'd feel on licking Blain? It wasn't there. Just a feeling of distaste at having fought and licked a member of his own ball club. The picture was all wrong because, as Marty saw it at the moment, nothing had been gained.

He waited until the second had removed the gloves and bandages. He stood up then to leave the ring, but before he had a chance to straddle through the ropes he heard a hoarse voice from the other corner.

"Marty." It was Blain.

Marty turned and stood poised, resentment sweeping through him. He didn't want any more of Blain just now. Blain called, "Come over here, will ya, guy? I'm still a little weak."

Marty started across the ring, moving slowly, unwilling to believe the thing he'd heard in Blain's voice. His incredulity was taxed still further when he saw the tired but friendly grin on Mugger's face. He was still distrustful as he stood before the pitcher. Sensing this, Blain said, "Relax. It's over, kid. For good I hope. I've tangled with you all I want to."

Marty stared. It was all he *could* do. Blain went on ruefully, "I have to learn the hard way. But I generally remember what I learn. I was wrong about you, Marty. You're no phony. You can play first base on my team any time."

Marty stared a little more, but a light of huge relief was growing in his eyes. His weariness dropped off. It was nice to be alive again. He finally found his voice and stammered, "Well—well, gosh, Mugger, I—I—" He bogged down, took a fresh start, and blurted, "Thanks, Mugger! Thanks a lot!"

"You haven't got anything to thank *me* for," grinned Blain. "I'm just lookin' out for my own hide, tryin' to make friends with you, so when I shoot off my mouth again you'll let me down a little easier. Want to shake on it?"

"You *bet* I do," grinned Marty, grabbing Blain's extended hand.

The Bantams had remained impartially silent

throughout the fight but now there was an outbreak of irrelevant chatter which indicated their relief and pleasure. They aimed a lot of it at Marty, and quite as much at Mugger Blain. Both men had grown in stature in the Bantams' eyes, and they let that fact be known. Marty caught the undertones and felt a warmth inside him. At last he was solid with the club. No doubt about it now.

# CHAPTER 16

The following days confirmed it, days filled with more solid satisfaction than Marty Shane had ever known before. His bat spoke loudly for him. It was the most effective press agent a man could possibly desire, and every hit that rattled off his war club made him more solid than ever with the fans.

They were all for him now. What if he did make an occasional fielding blunder? The fans learned to accept these errors as amusing jokes. It was the pounding of the horsehide that kept their interest in Marty Shane at fever heat.

It was a sour dose for Rudy Kemp to swallow, and he didn't swallow it with resignation. He kept his distance for the most part, but on their infrequent meetings Marty read the mean determination in Kemp's eyes. Kemp wasn't giving up. He was waiting for an opening. When he found it, he would jump into it with both feet.

But Marty didn't let it worry him. He could afford to shrug it off. He was riding the crest of a wave, and he enjoyed it. For the first time in his life he was a real big shot. When he walked down Main Street folks would point him out and say, "That's Shane." Fans greeted him with, "Hi, Marty, how's the boy?" Marty liked to flap his hand and say, "Not bad. Not bad at all."

He bought himself a secondhand convertible coupe, and rented a cottage down on the shore of Lake Erie. The only drawback to the cottage was that Rudy Kemp happened to be his next door neighbor, a hundred yards or so away, but Rudy's cottage was a shack compared to Marty's. Marty also had his Cloudbuster parked at a nearby airport. He found time to take occasional hops. It was the way to live.

There were a lot of fine people here along the beach, and most of them welcomed Marty as their guest. He did a considerable amount of his visiting at night, and the card games sometimes lasted pretty late. However, so long as his batting average didn't slump, Marty didn't worry about late hours.

Dinty and Jake Larkin shared the cottage with him, and Marty was surprised one day to find that Dinty was doing some of the worrying that Marty conscientiously avoided. The two of them were sitting on the beach one day, still wet from their morning swim.

"Still aiming for the big leagues, Marty?" Dinty asked abruptly.

"Huh?" said Marty vaguely. Then, "Sure. Why not?"

"You're getting sidetracked," Dinty told him bluntly. "And you seem to like it."

Marty considered this good-naturedly, admitting, "You're right about my liking it. Why shouldn't I? It's a great life, Dinty. Why kid myself? I'll never get this much fun out of big league ball. I'd be just another ball player in the big time, and I certainly don't need the dough."

Dinty let the sand run through his fingers. "Yeah," he said. "You'd be just another ball player—*if* a big league club would sign you. I doubt if any of 'em would. You're too weak around the bag, and you're making no effort to get better. Confound it, Marty, you've got half a dozen glaring faults."

175

"Name one," Marty challenged, slightly annoyed.

"Okay, the way you throw, for instance. You've got a good arm, but in order to control it you always have to have your left foot on the ground. It slows you up."

"Not much," insisted Marty stubbornly.

"Too much," said Dinty. "You ought to be able to start a hard peg while your left foot's still kicking out in its reach. By the time your left foot hits the ground to catch your weight, the peg ought to be under way. With you it's different. You have to anchor your left foot first before you can control the throw."

Marty shrugged and said, "Okay, you're probably right. I'll fix it up some day."

Dinty threw a handful of sand disgustedly to the ground.

"Let's skip it," he said shortly.

"Yeah, let's do," said Marty amiably.

But Dinty didn't follow his own suggestion. He said, as if talking to himself, "Why hasn't Lobo tried to cure you of some of your bad fielding habits?"

"Because he's smart," said Marty with confidence. "He's letting me save all my energy for batting, where it shows up best."

"You *believe* that?"

"What else is there to believe?"

"It's too deep for you to understand," said Dinty irritably, and let the matter drop.

When they went back to the house the phone was ringing. It was a party line, and they listened to be sure it was their number, two shorts. It was. Marty answered it, then gasped, "Who?"

The voice at the other end repeated, "This is Bender. I'm your brother. Remember?"

Something inside Marty tightened as his last contact with his brother came vividly to mind.

"Yeah," he said, "I seem to recall vaguely. Where are you?"

"Here in Buffalo."

"Huh?" jerked Marty. "What for?"

"Short vacation," Bender said. "We thought we'd like to see the Bantams play a game or so. We're on our way to a series with Chicago."

"Who's 'we'?" asked Marty.

"Miss Parker, the other part owner of the Quakers."

"The old maid?"

Bender hesitated, then said, "Yeah, the old maid. How about having lunch with us? Will you meet us at the Statler at twelve-thirty?"

"Okay," said Marty. "I'll be there."

He eased the phone back to its cradle, turned thoughtfully to Dinty Mead, and said, "That was my brother, Bender. He's stopping over here to see us play. Now why the deuce do you suppose he's doing that?"

Dinty grinned and said, "Seems obvious to me. He's here to look you over, guy. Maybe he needs a slugger. Who can tell?"

"Can you think of any other funny gags?"

Dinty shrugged. "It wasn't a gag. It just seems to add up, that's all."

A slow excitement crept into Marty. He tried to keep himself from taking Dinty's hunch with too much seriousness, but, as Dinty had said, it might add up, at that. At any rate it was Marty's chance to give his hard-boiled brother an eyeful. And, the thought pestered him, maybe Bender *did* need a slugger. He surely was familiar with Marty's present batting average of .430. Maybe—just maybe. But he shrugged it off and said with forced pessimism, "Naw. Bender wouldn't give me a job if I was Hal Chase. He just stopped by, hoping I'd get rattled and make a clown of myself. He'll find out."

"Well, good luck, anyway," said Dinty.

Marty drove into town for his luncheon date. Entering the lobby, he soon spotted Bender's square figure parked in a leather chair. In the chair next to Bender sat a young woman. Marty shot her a second glance. She was easy on the eyes. Bender got up and came to meet him. They shook hands with restraint; then Bender said, "Come on, I'll introduce you to our partner."

Marty didn't tumble to it right away. As they stopped before the attractive woman, Marty's first thought was, "Wow! The guy works fast."

Marty was still slow on the pickup when Bender said, "This is Alma Parker, Marty, the girl who owns the rest of our ball club."

"The—the—*who*?" stammered Marty weakly.

"The old maid," said Alma Parker soberly.

"Holy cats!" gasped Marty. "I—I thought—" He bogged down as the color sizzled upward from his collar.

Alma laughed. It had a reassuring sound. She extended her hand, which Marty grabbed clumsily, aware of its firm grip.

She said, "You're a very satisfactory person, Marty. I'm flattered."

Recovering fast, Marty grinned and said, "It was partly Bender's fault. He led me to believe you were a spinster."

"But I am."

"And obviously by choice," said Marty gallantly.

"Let's eat," said Bender practically.

It was a pleasant luncheon. Marty enjoyed it. He liked Alma Parker, thought she was swell, even though she was apparently several years his senior. Bender too seemed to be more human than Marty had known him for some time.

Everything went so smoothly that a mild suspicion began struggling in Marty's thoughts. He tried, in a half-hearted way, to pin it down, but didn't quite succeed. Not until the game that afternoon was almost ready to get under way did Marty isolate the thought that had been nagging him.

It happened during the Bantams' warm-up session in the field. Marty's logic began to function when he spotted Bender and Alma Parker in a box behind first base, and the blunt conclusion he reached teetered him back upon his heels. Bender was hoping to marry Alma Parker, hoping to get control of Alma's baseball stock, and hence, complete control of the ball club.

It was a jolt to Marty, and he didn't know quite why, except that it was further proof of Bender's hard-headed practicality, a quality Marty had always resented in his brother.

Marty had sense enough, however, not to brood upon it at the moment. One job at a time, and his present job was to unveil a brand of baseball which would make Bender's eyes pop out. It was important, vitally important. So Marty riveted his attention upon the game.

He managed to perform, during the warm-up session, in a manner he considered more than adequate. He fielded some snappy grounders, and none of his pegs were too wild for the other infield men to handle. So far so good.

The Bantams were tangling with the Jays that afternoon, a hard-hitting club of youngsters who could easily prove dangerous. Mercer was showing his respect for them by sending Mugger Blain out to the mound.

Blain had been improving steadily, and Marty had never seen him look better than he looked today. The Jays, sluggers that they were, were being pitched to by a master. Blain paced himself carefully, eased up when he had the chance, and bore down in the clutches. What hits the Jays collected were scattered and not dangerous. Blain had things well under control.

Marty didn't resent this for Blain's sake, but was a little disappointed on his own count. Blain's mound work did not permit Marty the fielding chances he would have liked. His war club, however, was still his pal. He clouted in two runs on his first trip to bat, giving Bender something to think over.

In the top of the fifth Marty had a brilliant fielding chance, and he made it good—half of it at any rate. The Jays had managed to work a man around to third, with one out. The batter drilled a line drive toward right field, but Marty sailed high into the air and pulled it down with a one-handed circus catch.

The man on third was halfway home when Marty made his peg to third. The throw was a little high, over Gordon's head in fact, which was too bad in view of the fact that the runner had time to come back, touch the bag, then score. Blain almost blew his top, but not quite. He showed a masterful restraint. He glanced at Marty, grinned painfully, and let it go at that.

Marty felt pretty bad about it, but not too bad considering the fact he had already clouted home the two runs that left the Bantams in the lead. He felt even less bad about it when he opened the bottom of the fifth with a screaming double, reached third on a fielder's choice, then scored after the catch of a long fly.

He had another chance at bat in the bottom of the seventh. The game was already sewed up with a 6–1 score, but Marty had no thought of easing up. He whammed a homer with two men on. Let Bender chew on that one for a while, Marty thought. The Bantams coasted home, and Marty was well satisfied with what he'd done.

He talked to Bender after the game, but learned nothing from his brother's noncommittal attitude. Bender told him he and Alma Parker were heading for Chicago the following morning. He invited Marty to dinner with them, but Marty refused, not too diplomatically. Bender shrugged.

# CHAPTER 17

That evening at the cottage, Marty and Dinty were alone. Jake Larkin was attending his weekly Grange meeting at a small town just outside Buffalo.

"Baseball players are fine people," Jake had explained. "But I think like a farmer, and I always will. I've just *got* to talk crops and livestock now and then, and these farmers that meet at the Grange sure know their stuff."

Dinty had his nose in a detective story, but when Marty kept prowling around the cottage instead of leaving for his usual late visit with the neighbors, Dinty put aside his magazine and said, "What's eatin' you?"

"Nothing," said Marty irritably.

Dinty snorted, but before he could reply, the phone rang, two shorts. Marty grabbed it and said, "Hello."

He listened stiff-faced for a moment, then said, "So what? I'm glad to hear it. The guy deserves it." He replaced the phone, turned to Dinty, and said briefly, "Bender just bought Mugger Blain for the Quakers."

"The deuce you say!" jerked Dinty. Then slowly, "I guessed wrong. It was Mugger he came to see. I'm sorry, Marty."

"There's nothing to be sorry for," said Marty gruffly. "Mugger earned the chance. He'll make good."

Dinty reached for his magazine, then checked the motion of his hand. He studied Marty's set expression for a moment before saying, "You shouldn't be sore at Bender, Marty. He's a businessman."

"Businessman!" rasped Marty. "*I'll* say he's a businessman! He wouldn't let anything stop him on a business deal—and I'm not griping because he didn't buy me instead of Mugger."

185

Dinty thought this over carefully and shrewdly, then came up with the answer. "I guess you're talking about Alma Parker."

Marty's head jerked up. "How did you know *that?*" he demanded, but didn't give Dinty time to answer. "Sure, that's who I'm talking about," he admitted loudly. "Why not? Bender's after her stock in the club. Any dope could figure that out."

"Have you fallen for the girl yourself?" asked Dinty quietly.

Marty pulled up short. He stared at Dinty, but took time to give the matter careful thought, as if it were an entirely new idea.

Finally he said, "No, I'm sure I haven't. She's older than I am, and not my type. The point is that she's a perfectly swell person, and if Bender pulls a shindy on her like that, I'm going to beat the tar out of him."

Dinty said, "Ease up, and think *this* over. Has it occurred to you that Bender might be in love with her, and that she might be in love with Bender? Such things *do* happen," he added dryly.

Marty thought this over and felt silly. He looked a bit bewildered as he eased himself into a chair. He admitted finally, "No, I hadn't thought of that." He hauled in a deep breath, studied his toes, and said, "I guess there's something wrong with me. Maybe I'm just a mug." He raised his eyes to Dinty's and said, "Honestly, I wish I didn't feel that way about Bender. It's all wrong. I know that much. He's probably a better man than I am, but admitting it doesn't seem to help. He simply rubs me the wrong way, and there doesn't seem to be anything I can do about it."

"Tough," said Dinty.

"Yeah, it's tough," admitted Marty.

Dinty changed the subject. "Lobo must have gotten a whale of a big price for Mugger Blain. He could have cinched the pennant with Blain and Jake. It'll put a big load on Jake."

"He can carry it," said Marty absently. "He's found himself. He'll be better before the season ends than Mugger ever was."

"Yeah," said Dinty. Then to make conversation he said, "Birch and Mark and Johnson are also coming along fast. Lobo's got a gold mine in his pitchers."

Marty wasn't listening. Sensing it, Dinty asked, "Going out tonight?"

"Huh?" asked Marty. "No. Nor any other night."

"You kiddin'?" Dinty asked, astonished.

Marty shook his head. "I'm going to learn to play first base," he said. "Bender's visit did me a lot of good, after all. I've got to show the guy, that's all. I've been a chump."

Marty's intentions were grade A. It was his firm resolve to improve his fielding to the point where he could catch the eye of big league ivory hunters. He had finally tumbled to the fact that fielding was important.

His conviction, however, was upset with a violence which shook it loose from its foundation. He had scarcely readjusted himself to the prospect of a long uphill fight when the world was suddenly dropped into his lap. It took place only a few days after Bender's visit. Mercer called Marty to his office.

"I've got some news for you," said Mercer.

"What is it?" Marty asked.

"I've sold you," Mercer told him bluntly.

Marty stared incredulously. Then a hollow feeling started forming in his stomach as a horrible conviction came upon him. Mercer was having his revenge on Bender Shane at last. He was undoubtedly passing Marty on to some grubby little club. Marty hauled in a deep breath for the blowoff when Mercer added, "To the majors."

Marty teetered on his feet as if he'd been clipped with a blackjack. His eyes bugged out. Then suddenly he snarled, "Don't kid me, Mercer!"

"Shucks, Marty, I wouldn't kid you," Mercer said. "I'm handing you straight stuff. You're in the big time now."

Marty sank into a chair. "What club?" he demanded hoarsely.

"I've sold you to the Rangers."

Marty battled his emotions for a while, and finally steadied them. It was a colossal dose of news to swallow in one lump, but he finally managed it. The Rangers were in the same league with the Quakers, another break of luck Marty had scarcely dared to hope for. His thoughts were still too jumbled to express in words, and Mercer, probably sensing this, went on, "The Rangers, of course, are still wallowing in the cellar, which is the reason you got a chance with them. They need somebody who can hit the ball out of the infield."

"That's me," said Marty with a sudden surge of dizzy confidence.

"That's what I told 'em," Mercer said.

"When do I leave?"

"They want you right away. I figure you'll make good, of course, but if you don't, Marty, I've got you protected by a clause I added to the contract. If by any chance they *do* want to sell you back to the minors, I get first chance at you for the price they paid me."

Marty nodded. He said, his confidence still high, "Looks like you've seen the last of me."

"I hope so, Marty, for your sake. However, there's a small string tied to the deal."

"What is it?" Marty asked suspiciously.

"Well, because you're part owner of a rival club in the same league with the Rangers, the Commissioner has ruled that you'll have to get rid of your Quaker stock before you join the Rangers."

Marty stiffened in his chair. This was an angle he had not anticipated, and he didn't like it. The Quaker stock meant a lot to him. It was his principal source of income, his guarantee of a comfortable old age. If he had the money in one lump sum right now, he might go through it. He knew himself.

But gradually it dawned upon him that crashing the big leagues was infinitely more important at the moment than mere finances. Wonderingly he pondered this, forced finally to accept the fact that baseball now was all that mattered.

"I'll sell it," he said quietly.

Mercer rubbed a hand across his desk top thoughtfully, then said, "I have some friends with dough. I have some tucked away myself. We could form a pool and take it off your hands."

A bell rang in the back of Marty's mind. It had a warning note which roused a sudden surge of indignation. He had not planned, as yet, to whom he'd sell the stock, but certainly he had no intention of letting Lobo Mercer get his hands on it.

And then a strong conviction hit him. It galled

him but he couldn't throw it off. The Quaker stock, he knew, must stay in the Shane family. Just why, he couldn't quite figure out, but that's the way it was. He'd have to offer it to Bender. He'd have to give his brother full control. The thought went far toward souring his elation, but he said, "Sorry, Lobo, but my brother rates first chance at it."

Mercer shrugged and said, "Of course." Then getting to his feet to close the interview, he stuck out his hand. "Good luck, Marty! Keep sluggin' 'em and you'll stay up there."

There was a curtain over Mercer's eyes which Marty couldn't penetrate. He shook hands, wondering what thoughts were curdling in Mercer's mind. And when Marty headed for the door, he felt a cold spot just between his shoulder blades, the spot where Mercer's eyes were probably fastened.

# CHAPTER 18

Marty Shane felt rather funny about breaking his good news to Dinty and Jake, particularly Dinty, who also rated a chance at the big leagues. Both men, however, were unreservedly elated at his good fortune, and their unselfish feelings on the matter made Marty feel a whole lot better.

"Will you fly out?"Dinty asked.

"No," said Marty. "I'm going to leave the crate in Buffalo until I'm sure I'm good enough to stay upstairs."

Marty called Bender on the phone that evening

to arrange for the transfer of the stock. Bender congratulated him as if he meant it, and Marty tried hard to believe that Bender's acquisition of the stock was not the only reason for his friendly tone. Nevertheless, Marty was relieved when it was over. He could now concentrate on the job ahead of him, the pleasant task of batting his way to glory with the Rangers.

He took time out to have a laugh over how he'd let himself get panicky about fielding. Great fielding was all right in its place, but nothing could take the place in baseball of great sluggers. Who was the highest paid big leaguer in history? A slugger—the Bambino. That's what the majors wanted, what they paid for—slugging.

His spirits were still looping in the stratosphere when he joined up with the Rangers. He had brains enough, of course, to keep his feelings under wraps, and to assume the outward humbleness of a raw rookie. But he didn't feel that way inside. He had the itch to try his war club on some big league pitching.

He had almost overlooked, in his excitement, a fact of great significance to him. He reported to the Rangers at a time when they were locked in a four-game series with the Quakers, who were still on their western swing.

Marty didn't have any fantastic dreams about

being tossed into the Ranger lineup as soon as they found a uniform to fit him, but he did concede the possibility he might be sent in as a pinch hitter. After all, that's what they'd bought him for, to hit.

The manager of the Rangers, Mike Callahan, was a man with lots of wrinkles and lots of baseball experience, who had been handicapped of late years through lack of funds. He had the reputation of being a fine old guy, who treated his men right and got the most out of them. Marty liked him right away. After shaking hands, Callahan said, "Glad to have you with us, Marty. I hope you've brought along the batting power we need."

"I hope I have, sir."

"I think we can iron out some of your fielding wrinkles."

"I guess I've got some to be ironed out."

Callahan rubbed a worried hand across his chin and said, "I intended to break you in by degrees, but I'm going to have to put you in the lineup right away—this afternoon, in fact."

Marty swallowed the quick lump of alarm which found its way unexpectedly into his throat, "How—how come I'm going in so soon?" he asked.

"We had an accident in yesterday's game. Our first baseman, White, slid into second on a close play. He tangled with the Quakers' second baseman, Flint, and when the dust cleared away my boy had a busted ankle and Flint had a pulled ligament in his knee. Both boys'll be out for the rest of the season."

"Tough," said Marty.

"Yeah. And my other first baseman's laid up with stomach trouble, so I'll have to start you sooner than I'd planned. Your brother, I hear, is going in for his club."

"Oh," said Marty, feeling a strange tingle of excitement travel through his veins.

The tingle was still there when game time pulled around. Marty had made no effort to get in touch with Bender in the meantime. His reason for this, he conceded to himself, was somewhat on the childish side, but the fact remained he wanted to confront Bender in a big league uniform. It would place them on more equal terms than they'd ever been before, and Marty wanted it that way.

He got his white uniform with RANGERS splashed across the front, and he'd never felt so dressed up in his life. He felt like strutting, had a hard time, in fact, to keep from doing so. He met the other members of the club. They studied him curiously, of course, but otherwise seemed friendly.

He met Bender. Bender came over to him while the Rangers were lining up for batting practice. They shook hands, and Bender led the way back to the grandstand, where they leaned against an empty box.

"Kid, I'm mighty glad to see you here." Bender's tone was gruff, but not lacking in sincerity. Things might have been all right if he hadn't added, "I hope you stick."

The latter statement too was undoubtedly meant in the right way. The trouble was, Marty chose to place his own interpretation on it. He obeyed a perverse and completely illogical urge to make the most of the moment, to rub in the fact he was now in the big time, despite Bender's former statement that he lacked the stuff to get there. So he demanded pointedly, "And why shouldn't I stick?"

"No reason, kid," said Bender hastily. "Callahan usually knows what he's doing."

But Marty wouldn't let it drop. "*You* don't think I'll be around long, do you?" he demanded.

Bender began to show annoyance. "Let's wait and see," he said.

"How long are you prepared to wait?"

Bender wasn't geared to stand that sort of needling. His voice had an edge when he retorted, "Look, kid, I've tried to meet you more than halfway, but you're askin' for the facts. Frankly I *don't* think you'll last very long unless you get wise to yourself. That uniform you're wearing doesn't make you a major leaguer. There's more to it than that, and the sooner you find it out the better off you'll be. For my money you're still a rookie, and a doubtful one."

"I proved you were wrong once," snapped Marty. "And I'll prove it again."

"I hope you do," said Bender. "For the good of the family name. I'd hate to be ashamed of you."

"Don't hand me that tripe," said Marty harshly. "You've got what *you* want out of me. You've got my stock, and you control the Quakers. You'd like to see me booted back to the minors. Maybe you'd even like the chance to prove I'm not good enough to play in the same league with guys like you."

Bender studied him a long hard moment. "Maybe I would like the chance," he said quietly. "And maybe I'll get it."

He wheeled and walked away. Marty cooled off fast, feeling like a heel. Just why, he asked himself disgustedly, had he had to shoot his mouth off like that? Why had he had to stick his neck out? He'd acted like a spoiled stupid brat, and he was smart enough to know it.

He didn't have much time for self-recrimination, though, because Mugger Blain spotted him and came striding over. Marty was glad to see him. It made him feel less alone. He asked, after they'd shaken hands, "You working today, Mugger?"

"Nope. I'm still utility. But you're getting a nice break."

"I hope you're right," said Marty fervently. "Frankly, Mugger, I'm jumpy as a cat."

"So what? You'll get over it. Take it easy, kid, and good luck."

Blain's assurance helped. Marty managed, with an effort, to fasten his mind upon the game. Batting and fielding practice proved beneficial. He did all right in both, and his confidence came back, aided by the knowledge that this was the biggest moment in his life. He didn't dare to muff it. He didn't think he would.

The Rangers, humble tail-enders that they were, were invariably poison to the Quakers. It was one of those things, and the Ranger fans, knowing it, were always rabid when the Quakers came to visit them. The Rangers had won the first game of a four-game series. The Quakers had won the second. This was the third, and the hometown fans were sizzling.

They were also watching Marty Shane with open apprehension. Marty was aware of it, but didn't let it worry him. His concentration now was sound. The Rangers, despite the fact that he was still an unknown quantity, were mighty nice about it. They included him in their chatter as if he'd been on first base for months.

No fireworks developed in the top of the first inning. The Rangers had a husky right-hander on the mound by the name of Mule Shelly who almost always looked good against the Quakers. The first Quaker flew out to short right. The second grounded to the second baseman, Hobensack, who flipped an easy one to Marty in time for the out. Shelly sent the third man down swinging, and the Rangers came to bat.

They were faced by a rangy southpaw, Lefty Sack. He wasn't the Quakers' best hurler, but he was plenty good. He demonstrated this on the Ranger lead-off man, Jug Miller, right fielder.

Miller took a called strike, a pair of balls, fouled one off, and went down swinging on the fifth pitch. The second Ranger, Jim Cassen, center fielder, didn't do much better. He popped a high fly to the first baseman for the second out.

Marty came up next, well aware that third spot on the batting list was a complimentary assignment for a raw rookie. It didn't scare him. He had things under control by this time, and, so far as he was concerned, Lefty Sack was just another pitcher. The fact he was a southpaw made him all the more vulnerable to a right-handed hitter.

Marty soon found out, however, that Sack wasn't just another pitcher. His lazy, loose delivery was deceptive. The ball seemed to gain speed as it came, and when the first one fizzed across Marty's letters like a bazooka shell, it went for a called strike.

Marty felt a little silly. He took a better toe hold and sharpened his eyes. He refused the next one, which hooked in too close to him. Sack hadn't fooled him, and the umpire called a ball.

The third pitch also went for a ball, and Marty began to feel he was in pretty good shape. Then Sack fed him a sharp curve which had a bend to it like an orange rolling off a table. Marty broke his back on it, but didn't even get a smell of it. He waited out a high pitch, and found himself with a full count on his hands.

His nerves had been all right up to this point, but it suddenly struck him what was going on. It was a bad time for such a thought to grab him, a bad time for him to realize he was facing a big league pitcher for the first time in his life, and that the next pitch would tell the tale.

He had a sudden congested feeling that the next pitch would be the most important he had ever faced, that it carried a significance far beyond its actual importance. It suddenly became a symbol, a thing of mighty import. Marty was not a superstitious man, but he had his moment of panicky superstition now. He knew with shocking certainty that a strike-out at this time would color his entire big league career. His hands felt slippery on the bat.

Lefty Sack took lots of time. He left the mound and reached for the resin bag. It was a break for Marty. He stepped from the box, dusted his hands upon the ground, and found time to pull himself together.

He was almost back to normal when he faced Sack for the payoff ball. The southpaw wound up slowly, and let go. Marty figured the delivery for a hook to break across the outside corner of the plate. He covered the spot with his swing, and felt the bat meet horsehide.

It was probably the finest feeling he had ever known. He could tell from the feel that he hadn't really clouted it—but he hadn't struck out, either, which was all that mattered now.

His knees were rubbery with relief as he headed for first base, trying to beat out the high-bouncing grounder down to short. He didn't stand a prayer. The shortstop had his peg across to first while Marty was still three strides from the bag. He was out—but they hadn't *struck* him out.

His luck stayed with him as the game settled down to a cutthroat battle. Mule Shelly ran true to form, rising to the heights he usually reached against the Quakers. He held them to four scattered hits in the early innings, and was still going strong when the halfway mark was reached.

The Rangers, on the other hand, didn't seem to be able to get their eyes on Sack's deliveries. Sack had a fine hatful of tricks, and all of them were working well today. The Rangers pecked out three hits while the Quakers were getting four.

Marty, unfortunately, did not contribute any of the Rangers' hits. Having weathered the crucial moments of his first time at bat, he was ready now to collect a few impressive bingles. Lefty Sack, however, had other ideas on the matter.

When Marty faced him again in the bottom of the third, Sack handled him with due respect, but nevertheless efficiently. It began to dawn on Marty he'd never faced this sort of pitching in the past. It had the polish and high temper of fine steel. It was calculated, deadly—yet there were many pitchers better than Sack in the majors. Marty Shane began to feel belated awe.

He got another chunk of the ball, it is true, on his second trip to the plate, but Sack had not permitted him to put control or power behind it. Even so, it might have sneaked past a small-time second baseman for a hit. The difficulty was that Bender Shane was not small time. He was still hot. He possessed a surprising burst of early speed, together with uncanny instinct. He got across to field the grounder neatly, and to throw Marty out at first. Marty felt the sting of it.

The sting was relieved somewhat by a fielding chance which came to him in the top of the sixth. Both clubs were still looking for their first run, and the Quakers, at this time, had the chance to get a pair across. With two down, they had men on second and third. Bender Shane came up to bat with the chance to bang in two runs with a hit.

He almost did. He cut hard at the first offering, and connected solidly. The ball came off his bat in a fuzzy streak. It came at Marty—above his head. He jumped and reached for it. It was all he could do. From that point on the baseball gods took over.

They were, apparently, on Marty's side. The ball whammed dead center in the pocket of his mitt and stuck there as if riveted in place. Marty couldn't have dropped it if he'd tried. It was embedded.

Nevertheless, it was a circus catch, and he got full credit for it from the fans. They liked it. So did Marty. What he liked better, though, was the expression of disbelief on Bender's face as he pulled up halfway down the path. Marty had to grin significantly at him. He couldn't help it.

Bender said, "Nice catch, Marty," and let it go at that.

Marty tried to hatch more glory for himself when

he came to bat in the bottom of the sixth inning, but the best he could manage was a long fly to center field. It was not a hit, and it began to dawn on him his time was running out. It was not a pleasant thought.

He would probably have but one more chance at bat. If he didn't crash through with a hit then— the hair along his neck began to prickle, and his palms felt slightly clammy.

# CHAPTER 19

In the top of the seventh the Quakers cut loose with a three-hit rally, tying the wallops together in a way which brought across two runs. The local fans began to yowl, and the Rangers got the idea right away. They drilled in a pair of counters of their own, to make the score a 2–2 deadlock.

Nothing happened in the eighth, no runs, no hits, no errors. But in the beginning of the ninth, the Quakers got the bit between their teeth again. The first man walked, and Bender Shane sent him to third on a long single to right field.

Mule Shelly showed his courage then. He struck out the next two men to face him. He was still in a hole, however, with Nick Walsh, a powerful slugger, in the batter's box. Giving Walsh a pass would not have helped, because Kling, the man who followed him, was equally dangerous.

Walsh crashed into the first pitch. It went foul into the left field lower stands, missing a home run by a foot, the sort of blow to turn a pitcher's blood cold. Another Ranger pitcher was working hard in the bull pen.

Shelly took his stretch, looked around, and saw Bender taking a long lead off first. Marty caught the sign and jumped fast for the bag to take Shelly's throw. It was a nice peg, but Bender hooked into Marty's right, and Marty couldn't lay the ball on him.

Bender got up, slapped off the dust, and took another crazy lead. Shelly tried to catch him again, but Bender could move like a streak of lightning when he wanted to. Once more he hooked into the bag on Marty's right, and the umpire called him safe.

Bender said quietly, "A real first sacker would have nailed me that time, Marty."

Marty kept his mouth shut, but he had the cold conviction Bender hadn't kidded him. Bender took another crazy lead and pulled another throw, beating it again in the same manner, a compact hook-slide to Marty's right. He was forcing Shelly to make the trys at first, and Shelly didn't need much forcing. Any pitcher would rather catch a man off first than to pitch to a slugger like Nick Walsh with a man on third.

Bender pulled a fourth throw and slid in safely. He was making Marty look bad. Marty knew it, yet beneath his growing anger was the strong alarming hunch that there was something deeper and more dangerous to Bender's tactics than the mere business of making his brother look bad. Marty racked his brains, but couldn't find the answer. He didn't get it until Bender pulled the fifth peg from the pitcher.

This time Bender slid in on Marty's *left* side—and everything came loose at once. The runner on third was more than halfway home, running like a thief.

Marty started his throw to the plate, then, with paralyzing clarity, he understood his brother's strategy. For Marty, as Dinty Mead had pointed out to him, had never been able to get an accurate peg away without landing on his left foot first. But Bender now was sprawled upon the spot where Marty's left foot ought to land. Bender had figured this all out, and had flashed his signal to the man on third. It was a frame-up.

Marty did his best. He made his heave before he had the chance to put his left foot where he wanted it. The throw was wild. The catcher, Kelldare, couldn't even stop it. It went back to the boxes, and Bender ended up on second. The run, of course, came in. And the irony of the thing was even worse when Shelly struck out Walsh, leaving the Quakers with a one-run lead.

Marty led off in the ninth. With all the bitter longing of his soul he wanted a hit now—but didn't get it. Instead, he popped out to the shortstop, a fumbling little infield fly the shortstop could have caught in his hip pocket. The Rangers didn't score. They lost the game by the one run Marty had so generously handed to the Quakers.

It was the lowest moment of Marty's life, and it took every ounce of fortitude he had to face it. He tried to keep his chin up, to look the other Rangers in the eye, but it was hard.

The Rangers themselves were more than decent about the whole thing, and kindly old Mike Callahan made it as easy for Marty as he could. He managed to get in a few words before they entered the locker room.

"Don't take it so hard, Marty," he said. "This big-time stuff was probably just a little tougher than you expected. But you'll find yourself, son, and I'll do everything I can to help you."

Callahan kept his word in this, despite the fact he pulled Marty from the lineup on the following day. He shifted his men around, and the Rangers' right fielder ended up in the first base spot. He turned in a creditable performance, even though the Quakers won.

Marty, in the following days, was given some intensive coaching in the art of covering the first sack. He did not master all the fine tricks of the job immediately, but he remembered them, worked hard, and began to show improvement.

His improvement, unfortunately, was not rapid enough to forestall the rabbit punch Fate had in store for him. Callahan called Marty to his office one day and broke the news without pre-amble.

"I'm sorry, Marty, mighty sorry, but I've got to let you go. I'm running a business, son, and I've got to run it the best I can. I've signed a first base-man from Los Angeles by the name of Brent. He's a first-rate fielder, and a fine hitter. I'm sorry, Marty. You've got the stuff, and if you keep on plugging, you're a sure bet for the majors. Don't quit fighting, son."

So Marty Shane went back to the Bantams. He felt like crawling back, but the feeling wore off before he got there. He fought it off with all the strength he had, and the effort he exerted brought compensating factors. It included, among others, a new clarity of insight.

He could understand now what Lobo Mercer had done to him, the sly vindictiveness which Lobo had exerted, together with Marty's own pigheaded self-importance which Mercer had employed skillfully. It seemed incredible to Marty that he hadn't tumbled to it sooner.

The whole business was following a pattern Mercer had conceived. He had, to start with, been deliberate in his failure to correct Marty's fielding faults. It had been almost inevitable that some major club, impressed by Marty's batting average, would sign him up and would learn too late of his indifference to the art of fielding. Mercer, at any rate, had gambled shrewdly along those lines, and the gamble had paid off.

Marty Shane had had his brief taste of the majors, and had fizzled out like a damp fuse. He'd been kicked back into the minors, labeled as a failure, subjected to the ignominy of being tagged as a cluck who couldn't make the grade. Mercer had taken his roundhouse swing at the Shane tribe and had scored a knockdown in the opening round.

But not a knockout. Marty Shane was dangerous now, more dangerous than before, because he was becoming tempered in the furnace of experience. His rage was cold and steady, but controlled by common sense.

Batting Mercer's teeth in wouldn't help. Being sullen wouldn't help him either. He had to pick up where he'd left off with the Bantams and their fans. If he used his head, it shouldn't be too difficult. He got off to a good start by clearing the first big hurdle—which was Mercer.

Mercer's first words were, "I'm sorry, Marty. You got a rotten break." The glitter in his eyes belied the sorrow in his tone.

Marty kept his temper under wraps. He was learning fast. He managed a rueful smile and said, "Shucks, Lobo, I just wasn't good enough. Those guys up there are tough. I need some more experience."

The curtain dropped before Mercer's eyes. He was puzzled. He couldn't reconcile himself to Marty Shane's submissiveness. But he said heartily, "Well, Marty, you'll get experience, starting now. I'm putting you right back in the lineup."

"Gee, thanks," said Marty.

Mercer stared at him suspiciously, then said, "You're welcome."

Marty asked, "Are Dinty and Jake still living in the cottage out by the lake?"

"They're still there."

"Well," said Marty, "I guess I'll go out and see if they'll take me back."

He didn't doubt for a moment that Dinty and Jake would be mighty glad to see him. The thing that upset him some was the probable nature of the reunion. It was bound to be embarrassing for everybody, Marty reasoned, and he didn't know quite how to go about it. He finally decided to barge in unannounced, and let matters take their course. The idea was to get it over with as soon as possible. So he walked into the living room and found Dinty there alone, reading a mystery magazine as usual.

Dinty glanced up, said, "Hi, Marty," casually, then tapped the magazine. "They got the guy tied up in an abandoned mine. Between him and the entrance they got a half a dozen sticks of dynamite. They lit a long fuse and ran away and left the poor sucker there alone. He's watching the flame creep nearer and nearer the dynamite. When it goes off it'll blow down the roof of the mine and leave him trapped."

"Two to one he makes it." Marty grinned.

Dinty shook his head doubtfully. "I think they got him this time."

Jake Larkin appeared in the doorway, blocking it with his big frame.

"Hi, Marty," he said. "I got a new pet, Anna-bella, a raccoon. She's almost tame. Come out and see her."

"Yeah," said Dinty. "Go ahead. I want to finish this."

So Marty followed Jake outside, feeling warm and comfortable inside.

The other Bantams made things just as easy for him. He fitted back into his old spot like a cog in a gear. The fans were glad to see him. So were the men. Marty tried to keep it that way, tried to temper his new grimness with geniality.

In the meantime he settled down to work, real work. Mercer was still cagey with suggestions about fielding, but Marty didn't need suggestions now. He put into practice what he'd learned with the Rangers. He was a glutton for the work, and as he mastered the fine points he began to like it.

His fielding play improved, as it was bound to, and with improvement came the belated development of instinct for the play around first base. The hits kept booming off his bat, and as the summer rolled along the Bantam fans became hysterical about him.

The Bantams were battling for top billing with the Syracuse Colts. The two clubs were running neck and neck, and the fans of both teams were taking the matter very seriously. So were the teams themselves.

Jake Larkin had, by this time, more than justified Mercer's hopes. He had developed an explosive hook which he could now control as accurately as he could control his straight one. In recent games he had licked the Colts each time he faced them.

The Colts were leading by a half a game at the time the Bantams were scheduled for a three-game series in Syracuse. Mercer made no secret of the fact he would start Jake Larkin in the opener, determined to put the Bantams in the lead again without delay.

On the night before the Bantams were to leave for Syracuse, Marty Shane was playing solitaire. Dinty tried to read a mystery story, but kept glancing at the clock. He finally tossed the magazine irritably aside and said, "He ought to be here."

"He probably got himself in a long-winded argument about contour farming and forgot what time it was."

"I don't think so," said Dinty flatly. "Nothing would keep Jake from getting his ten hours' sleep before a game. That Grange meeting ends at eight-thirty, and he's always back here by nine. It's nine-forty-five right now. Something's wrong. Let's go after him."

"He's got my car," Marty pointed out.

Dinty left his chair and started to pace the floor. "I don't like it," he said bluntly. "Something's wrong."

"What *could* be wrong?" asked Marty, playing a red six on a black seven.

"How do *I* know?" Dinty snapped. "I've got a hunch, that's all, the strongest one I've had in years. With Jake pitching we're a cinch to win tomorrow. The odds'll be five to one with us. But if Jake doesn't pitch—and someone had taken advantage of those odds—well, figure it out yourself."

"For Pete's sake!" said Marty, playing a card impatiently. "You've been reading too many detective stories."

"Maybe I have," admitted Dinty. "But I'm worried now. And you know I don't get out on a limb very often."

Marty did know this. As a result, some of Dinty's uneasiness transmitted itself to Marty. He scooped his cards into a pile and looked at Dinty.

"It's really more than a hunch, Marty," Dinty said. "Rudy Kemp's been acting mighty funny lately."

"Kemp," scoffed Marty. "He may be a louse, but he hasn't got the guts to be a crook."

"Maybe not," said Dinty. "But I can't get him out of my mind. You know I drop in at his cottage

215

every now and then, and for the past few days he's been jumpy as a flea. He's scared of something. Plenty scared."

The phone gave three sharp rings, no more, as if someone had been waiting to grab the receiver off the hook. Dinty, with a quick gesture of decision, headed for the phone.

"That's not our ring," said Marty. "It's Kemp's."

"I know it," said Dinty grimly, reaching for the instrument. "It's what we detectives call wire tapping. It's perfectly legitimate when we're on a case."

Before Marty could protest further, Dinty lifted the receiver. He listened a moment, and his face went tight. It was pale with anger when he eased the phone back into its cradle.

"Don't tell *me* my hunches are no good," he said. "The guy at the other end told Rudy, 'It worked out fine. He's locked up tight. He won't pitch against the Colts.' Then Rudy squealed, 'Shut up, you lug! This is a party line!' The other guy said, 'Okay,' and hung up."

Marty digested this with mounting rage. He finally left his chair and started for the door.

"Where you goin'?" asked Dinty sharply.

"You know right well where I'm goin'," Marty answered.

"Hold on a minute," Dinty snapped. "You may beat it out of him and you may not. In either case he'll have you tossed in the clink. Then where'll *you* be for tomorrow's game?"

Marty took time to think it over, and the answer was rather obvious.

"All right," he conceded irritably. "Maybe you've got a better idea."

"I *will* have," said Dinty with great confidence. "Just gimme a little time to think."

He resumed his chair, sat back, and pondered. He was solving a case and thoroughly enjoying the experience. While Marty fidgeted and waited, he heard the front door of Kemp's cottage slam. Then came the sound of the roaring motor in Kemp's car. A moment later the reporter whizzed past on his way to town.

Dinty sat up and said, "Ah! I think that does it. He's gone to town to get plastered. Guilty conscience. I've almost got it now."

"Do you want your violin or your needle, Sherlock?" Marty asked him.

Dinty ignored the remark. "Now listen," he said excitedly. "Rudy's supposed to leave with the team tomorrow morning. If he misses that train he can't get another in time to get him there for the play by play he's got to send back to his paper. If he misses that train he'll be desperate, because his job's a little wobbly, anyway. He's been drinkin' too much lately."

"Very interesting," said Marty with elaborate patience.

"He'll have his usual skinful when he goes to bed tonight,"said Dinty as if he hadn't heard the comment. "He always sleeps late and depends on an electric alarm clock to wake him up. Now the chances are he'll be so cockeyed he won't even notice the time on that clock, and will merely set the alarm trigger. So if I sneak over there now and set the clock *back*, he'll get up an hour late and will miss the train."

He beamed at Marty, expecting commendation for his cleverness.

"Incredible!" breathed Marty. "You're colossal!"

"Well," defended Dinty, "I haven't finished yet. I can't expect an untrained mind like yours to follow me. But here's the payoff. I phone him from the station and tell him he's an hour late, that the train is pulling out without him. He's desperate, see? Then he looks out the window and sees you loafing on the beach. He rushes out to find out why *you* aren't on the train. You tell him you're flying to Syracuse in your own crate, and his problem is solved. So is ours when you get him in the air. You must know a few tricks which would make Rudy want to talk."

Marty thought this over, his face slowly cracking into a complimentary grin.

"You've got a brain like a jigsaw puzzle," he told Dinty. "You've dreamed up a beautiful fairy tale, but the crazy thing *might* work, at that. We'll give it a try at any rate. We haven't enough evidence to take to the police, so we'll have to do the best we can."

# CHAPTER 20

After Dinty had returned from adjusting Kemp's alarm clock, Marty brought up a point neither of them, in their enthusiasm, had considered.

"How about Lobo Mercer?" Marty asked. "Maybe he won't let me fly my crate to Syracuse."

"By golly, that's a thought," admitted Dinty. "Call him up. Don't tell him more than you have to. There's still a chance we may be out on a limb."

Marty got hold of Mercer on the phone. "Listen, Lobo," he said, "will you let me fly my crate to Syracuse tomorrow?"

"No."

Marty drew a long breath and went on. "It's important, Lobo. Jake didn't come back from Grange meeting tonight."

"*What?*" yelled Mercer with alarm. "What happened to him? Where is he?"

"We don't know," said Marty. "But we're pretty certain he's been shanghaied."

"Are you trying to be funny?" demanded Mercer.

"It's straight stuff, Lobo, so far as Dinty and I can figure it out. We've got a pretty good idea who did it, but we're not going to mention any names until we know for sure. We also think we've figured out a way to *be* sure. If we're right, I can locate Jake tomorrow morning, and fly him to Syracuse in time for the game. That's why I asked permission to come by air."

There was a moment's silence at the other end of the line. Mercer finally said, "Okay, Marty. Do the best you can."

Marty didn't sleep very well that night. His rest was fitful. He heard the noise of Kemp's return, the squeak of brakes, the slamming of the car door. He heard Kemp curse as he stumbled clumsily up the front steps. Marty checked the time. Two o'clock. Dinty had been right, thus far, in his calculations. Rudy Kemp was getting to bed late, and he was plastered.

Not only that, but Dinty's calculations continued to prove sound, developing with almost uncanny accuracy. When Dinty had left for the station on the following morning, Marty climbed into a bathing suit and went to the beach where he loafed around conspicuously in front of Kemp's cottage.

Shortly after ten o'clock, Kemp's door burst open and he came lumbering out, half dressed in his undershirt and pants. He started hastily toward Marty, but slowed down before reaching the beach, trying to show a reasonable composure. His eyes were bloodshot and his hands were shaking. He was in excellent condition for the plans Marty had in store for him.

"Hi, Marty," he said thickly.

"Hello, Kemp," said Marty without interest.

"Aren't you going to play in Syracuse today?"

"Sure, I'm going to play."

"How're you getting there?"

"I'm flying over. Lobo gave me permission."

Kemp ran a tongue across his lips. He said, "Look, Marty, I'm in a bad jam. I missed the train, and I've *got* to be there for the game. Let me go over with you. Will you?"

"Why should I?" demanded Marty, eyeing him with distaste.

"Okay, okay, I know how you feel about me," admitted Kemp. "But you'd be doing my paper, also the fans, a big favor if you'd get me there in time to send back my play-by-play report."

Marty considered this with ominous deliberation, but finally said, "All right, I'll be a sucker. We'll go to the airport in your car. It'll save me taxi fare. We'll leave as soon as I get dressed." He started for the house.

They reached the airport a short time later. When they got there, Marty was glad to see Kemp's nerves were still behaving badly. They showed further deterioration while the two men stood by, waiting for the motor to warm up. Kemp eyed the small plane with distrust, making it obvious he was not air-minded. But he was behind the eight ball now. He had to get to Syracuse by game time.

When Marty said, "Okay, she's warm enough; let's climb aboard," Kemp caught his breath, then gathered all his nerve to heave himself into the seat beside the pilot. Marty took the pilot's seat, then carefully checked his instruments and his controls. Satisfied, he taxied up the field and turned his plane into the wind.

"Ready?" he asked Kemp.

Kemp nodded stiffly. Marty eased the throttle open, and the small ship started down the field, gathering momentum swiftly as it rolled. The tail came up almost at once, but Marty held the stick well forward, keeping the wheels upon the ground until the plane gained more speed than it needed for the take-off.

He lifted it gently from the ground but held it level, about six feet off, until it had attained its maximum flying speed. Then he dragged the stick back sharply, and the plane swooped upward in a dizzy zoom that plastered the passengers against their seats.

It was sudden and unexpected. Rudy Kemp's breath rushed out in a high-pitched squawk. When Marty leveled the Cloudbuster at the top of the zoom, Kemp managed to say hoarsely, "Did you *have* to do that?"

"No," said Marty mildly. "But it's a lot more fun."

"Well, take it easy," pleaded Kemp.

Marty didn't answer.

A little later Kemp exclaimed, "You're headin' for Lake Erie! That's not the way to Syracuse!"

"Isn't it?" asked Marty.

"You know right well it isn't."

"Oh, well," said Marty pleasantly. "We've got a lot of time to spare."

He glanced at Kemp. The reporter was getting pale. He was doggedly silent, but paler still, when they flashed across the water of the lake. Niagara Falls was on their right, about ten miles away. The high white plume of its spray was visible beyond

Lake Tonawanda. When Marty banked in that direction, Kemp went rigid. He must have known by then that something most unpleasant was in store for him.

Marty eased the throttle and went into a long deliberate glide. The angle of the glide, unless the course was changed, would carry them above the thundering water of the falls—not more than twenty feet above.

But Marty didn't change the course. He kept on going down. And not until his purpose was assured did Rudy find his voice.

He blurted, "No! No, Marty! *No!*"

"Where's Jake Larkin?" Marty asked him quietly.

"Larkin? I don't know. I—I don't know. Climb out of here! We'll never make it!"

"We can try, can't we?" Marty asked.

The falls rushed closer as the plane dropped lower. Kemp's lips were moving, but he couldn't force the words between them. Just off the surface of Lake Tonawanda Marty leveled off and gave his plane full throttle. It leaped ahead, racing toward the drop-off of the falls beyond which was the thundering abyss of tortured water.

They flashed across the brink. Air currents from below rushed up to toss the small plane violently. It danced and quivered in the air, while Marty grinned and handled the controls with careful understanding. He'd been across the falls before in this same plane. He knew what it would do. He also knew what *he* could do.

Kemp didn't. His voice came jerking out in squeals of terror. He was rigid, frozen in his seat when the air smoothed out, and Marty climbed for altitude.

"Where's Jake?" asked Marty patiently.

"I—I don't know," managed Kemp.

"Too bad," said Marty. "I'd sure like to find him."

He banked and started back around the falls. Reaching Lake Tonawanda, he made another turn. He headed toward the falls again and went into a glide.

"No!" Kemp pleaded. "No! No!"

"Yes," said Marty pleasantly. "I think it's fun. We'll shave it closer this time."

Kemp's face was now a pastel shade of green. He bleated, "No! Don't do it! I can't stand it!"

"It's up to you," said Marty. "Where is Jake?"

Kemp's nerves collapsed. "Turn back!" he blubbered wildly. "Turn back! I'll tell you where he is."

"I thought you would," said Marty as he leveled off and wheeled his plane around.

He climbed to a couple of thousand feet, then circled back above dry land while he waited for

Kemp to pull himself together. It took so long that Marty finally turned on him.

"Start talking," he ordered.

Kemp made the effort, but his voice was still unsteady.

"He's locked in a shed on an empty farm five miles east of Buffalo. I think I can find it from the air."

"How did he get there?"

"I—I arranged it." He was silent for a moment, then the words began to tumble out. "I *had* to do it. I was in a jam, a bad one. I got hooked up with a bunch of professional gamblers. They took me to the cleaners, all my cash, then hung a lot of I.O.U.s on me. I couldn't pay 'em back. They got tough. I was scared. Then they said if I could fix it up so Jake wouldn't pitch the first game against the Colts, they'd make a cleanup and give me back my I.O.U.s. I had to do it, Shane. I *had* to."

"And what'll you do now?" asked Marty. "After Jake wins the game today?"

Kemp groaned. "I'm through. I'll have to run for it."

"How sad," said Marty pleasantly. "I'm sure we'll miss you, Kemp."

They found the farm after a short search. Marty circled it a few times and spotted a smooth field where he could land. He brought the plane down

227

gently. The two men left the cabin. Kemp's knees gave way. He sat upon the ground while Marty headed for the buildings.

"Jake!" Marty yelled when he got there.

A muffled answer led him to a small windowless shed. He lifted the bar which held the door, and Jake came out, blinking against the light and looking sheepish.

"You're pretty old," said Marty sternly, "to be playing games like this."

"Yeah," said Jake, knuckling the stubble on his chin with deep embarrassment. "I'm sure a hick. But shucks, Marty, the guy *looked* like a farmer, and he said he had a prize heifer out here that he'd turned down two thousand dollars for. He said he'd give me a quick look at it, and bring me right back to town. I sure wanted to see that heifer. He said it was in this shed. I went in ahead of him, and he slammed the door and locked it."

"Get any sleep?" asked Marty.

"Oh, sure. Good sleep, on a pile of straw." He looked around and frowned. "This farm's *deserted*. I couldn't tell that last night, because it was dark. He couldn't have put it over on me if I'd known the place was empty." Then he asked curiously, "How'd you find me, Marty?"

Marty told him briefly, giving Dinty full credit for his deductions.

"Pretty smart," said Jake with proper awe. "Yes, sir, pretty smart."

They went back to the plane. Marty and Jake climbed in, ignoring Kemp. They left him sitting on the ground—the last they ever saw of him.

They flew to Syracuse, and landed there with time to spare. Jake won his opening game against the Colts, then the Bantams went ahead to win the series.

They looked good as the season rolled along, and Marty Shane kept plugging hard, giving baseball everything he had. He was good now and he knew it. There was no longer smugness to the knowledge, yet he couldn't help but wonder, now and then, why the majors didn't ask for him again. However, he always thrust the thought aside and kept on working.

The call inevitably came. It had to. Marty sensed it when Mercer called him to the office in late August. Something told Marty this was it, but he was not prepared for the full force of the avalanche. He might have guessed, though, from the fact that Mercer's mask was off. His face was ugly, his eyes mean. He spat out the words as if they were bitter.

"I've got to sell you to the Quakers."

Marty's knees suddenly went weak. Of all the sixteen big league clubs, the Quakers was the last he'd believed would buy him.

"The—the Quakers?" he repeated hoarsely.

"You heard me. Bender took an option on you as soon as the Rangers released you."

A tingling pleasure found its way into Marty's veins. He couldn't figure the business out, but one thing at least was clear.

He said with a tight grin, "And you didn't think he'd ever pick up the option. Did you? You didn't think that I'd improve enough."

Lobo Mercer merely glared, and Marty said softly, "You're a louse, Mercer. A dirty louse. Do you hear me, Mercer?"

Mercer heard him. He came halfway from his chair, then eased back slowly as he read the thing in Marty's eyes. Marty stared him down, then turned contemptuously and left the office.

# CHAPTER 21

Marty hated to say good-by to Jake and Dinty, but the parting was made easier by their honest pleasure at his success. It was a comfort, too, to know that both of them would soon be playing in the majors. They had the stuff. No doubt about it. They were on their way.

Marty entered another office three days later— Bender's. Marty still felt there was a catch somewhere to the transaction, and his suspicions must have shown. It's possible that Bender noticed this, but his face told nothing as he left his desk to shake hands with his brother.

"Well, Marty," he said, "you're back in the big time again, and my scouts all tell me you're here to stay."

"I hope so," Marty said. Then curiously, "But why did *you* buy me? You've got Rube Harlow who's one of the best first sackers in the game."

"True enough, but he's the only good man I've got for the position, and I've got to cover all the angles. We're hot this year, and we ought to cop the league flag. That means a crack at the big bunting, and I want to keep all the holes plugged."

Thinking it over, Marty said with low enthusiasm, "Looks like I've got a lot of bench-warming ahead of me."

"You probably have," said Bender, the challenge in his tone asking Marty what he was going to do about it.

There was also a flat finality to Bender's attitude which established their present relationship to each other without question. Bender was club manager, and Marty was nothing but a rookie, a fact Bender had no intention of letting him forget.

Marty sensed this, and found the self-control to accept it. He said, "Okay, Bender. You're the boss."

"I've *got* to be, kid," said Bender quietly.

He made it obvious in the days that followed. He ran the club with an iron hand as the Quakers settled down to stage their homestretch sprint. He was tough, but fair. Marty had to admit this, even though it griped him.

He had to admit also that there wasn't a Quaker on the team who wouldn't cut off his own leg for Bender Shane. It puzzled Marty, because he couldn't arouse the same feeling in himself. Bender treated him with unnecessary casualness, Marty felt, even though he understood the motive. Bender was leaning over backward not to show favoritism to his brother, but he was leaning back too far, Marty believed.

There was also the matter of Alma Parker. She attended all the home games, sitting in a box behind first base. Marty had spoken to her, but not at length. He still felt she was a fine person, but he felt awkward in her presence, a bit resentful of Bender's possessive attitude toward her, an attitude which appeared directly aimed toward matrimony.

Marty tried to be fair about it, but the thought persisted still that Bender's interest in her was induced by all the Quaker stock she owned. Marty wasn't too proud of these deductions, but they nagged him just the same, as a small added burden to his accumulating troubles.

He fought against his discontent and fretfulness as the Quakers battled hard to hold their slender margin as league leaders. The Boston Hawks, hot as a blowtorch flame, were right on the Quakers' tail. It was still anybody's race for the league flag.

Bender, it was true, didn't allow Marty to go stale. He kept him busy in practice sessions. He even let him make an occasional brief appearance in the lineup, but these brief moments only intensified Marty's discontent. He knew he was completely in the wrong to let it bother him. He simply couldn't help it. Rube Harlow, the regular first sacker, was much too good to be replaced.

As a result, the feeling of frustration grew in Marty. He could not feel he was an actual member of the team. He was homesick for the Bantams. He tried, but failed, to share the mounting tension in the Quaker ranks. He felt he was losing something of tremendous value. He made an honest effort, but he couldn't capture it.

Marty was still outside looking in when the season surged toward its dramatic close. No playwright could have written a more smashing climax. The Quakers, leading the Hawks by a single game, played host to the Boston team in a final four-game series.

The Hawks lashed out to win the first game, tying the Quakers for first place. It was Mugger Blain who pitched the Quakers into the lead again with a 4–2 victory. The Hawks came through in the third game to sew things up again. One game remained—the game to decide the winner of the flag.

Marty had watched all three games from the bench, phlegmatically. His lack of emotion really scared him now. Something was wrong with him, desperately wrong. Had he been mistaken all along in his belief that he was suited for the game of baseball? It was not a pleasant thought, but it haunted him now.

When he showed up for the final game he found a sober, worried bunch of Quakers in the dressing room. Mugger Blain came up to him and said, "Bender wants to see you in his office, Marty."

Belated excitement began to stir in Marty. He hurried to the office, where he found Bender in his baseball togs pacing up and down in stockinged feet. His face was grim. He said, "Rube Harlow picked today to get a taxi door slammed on his hand. He may be through for the season. You'll take his place."

Marty weathered the shock with confused emotions. He didn't know exactly how he felt. Elation slowly took the upper hand.

"A world series," he said unbelievingly. "A world series if we win today."

Bender's face, if possible, went harder, a defensive hardness. He said tightly, "Not for you, Marty.

You're not eligible. Your purchase papers weren't signed in time, not until a day after the first of September deadline. I'm sorry, Marty."

Marty stared at him. Then he felt his anger coming at him in an ugly wave. He couldn't check it. It gathered up his grievances like flotsam, swamped him with them. He wasn't reasoning at the moment, merely letting his emotions have their way.

"So that's the angle," he said coldly. "You wanted to make sure I wouldn't get a shot at the world series. You *still* don't think I'm good enough to play with guys like you, so you deliberately fixed it so you couldn't use me, even if you needed a first baseman."

The words made sense to Marty in his present frame of mind. It seemed like sound reasoning to him. He threw his logic triumphantly at Bender, but Bender made no comment on it.

The color slowly drained from Bender's face, but he controlled his voice. "Have it your own way, Marty. You can play today or you can warm the bench, whichever suits you best."

"I'll play," said Marty tautly.

He wheeled about and stamped from Bender's office. Play? You *bet* he'd play. He'd play with every ounce of skill and brains he had. And if the Quakers won this game, he told himself, his brother would be sadder and wiser. Bender Shane would wish with all his heart that he could use him in the series just beyond. And Bender could blame no one but himself.

The Quakers looked good in the practice session, almost too good. They made almost too much noise, showed too much pep as they tried to steam themselves up with a confidence they didn't feel. They kept worried eyes on Marty, watching him intently when he fielded grounders. Marty did well. He was efficient, poker-faced, mechanical, but the worries of the Quakers were not entirely eased. Marty could sense it. It amused him.

The game finally started with the Quakers in the field. Bender was still holding down the keystone sack. He had been playing top-flight ball since the injury to his regular second baseman. The Quakers' ace, Brad Logan, was on the mound. The Hawks had licked him in the opener, and Logan was out to prove they couldn't do it twice. The park was jammed with rabid fans.

Brad Logan bore down from the start. He sent the lead-off man down swinging. The second batter lobbed a feeble foul behind third base for the out. The third Hawk waited out a full count, then watched the payoff pitch as Logan sneaked it across the corner of the pan for the third strike.

The Quakers did not make out much better in their half of the inning, because the Hawks also started their pride and joy, Gil Hardwick. Hardwick, too, looked good. Jim Holt, Quaker shortstop, grounded out to second. Jug Coburn, right fielder, popped out to short, and Hap Grady, center fielder, whiffed.

The Hawks got their bats on the ball a couple of times in the second, but not dangerously. Marty made the third out on a peg from Holt, but it was a clean throw, and Marty was not called on to show any of his newfound skill.

He had his first chance at bat in the bottom of the second. Hockman, the left fielder, led off and drew a walk. Marty came to the plate ready to clout the cover off the ball, but Bender signed him to lay down a bunt. Marty swallowed his disappointment, liked the looks of the second pitch, and nudged it down the third base line. The third baseman came in fast, scooped up the ball, made a running throw and nailed Marty at first. Bender flied out to left, and Lutton, the Quaker third baseman, grounded out to first. No runs.

The third and fourth innings were uneventful, but the tension mounted as both pitchers continued to control the show. The tension was upon the Quakers tighter than it was upon the Hawks, because the Quakers still had the unknown quantity, Marty Shane, to worry over. It pleased Marty. He wanted them to worry. It would make his final satisfaction more complete.

In the top of the fifth, however, something happened to ease the Quakers' worries. The lead-off Hawk got to Logan for a bingle into left. The next Hawk sacrificed the runner down to second. The third poled a long fly back to the wall in right field. Coburn pulled it down, but the man on second base reached third by a whisker after the catch.

With a pair of outs, the infield played deep. The fourth Hawk to face Logan banged a sizzling grounder just inside the third base line. Ken Lutton made a magnificent running stop, but his peg to first was hurried.

It looked like a wild throw in the dirt to the right of the bag, but Marty had the reach and stretch of a rubber band. He pulled off a one-handed, backhanded pick-up, and managed to keep his right foot on the bag. The runner was out by half a stride. The run which crossed the plate did not count, and the Quaker fans went wild.

The effect on the Quakers themselves, however, was the thing which amused Marty most. As he headed for the dugout they clustered around him as if they'd found a gold mine. Marty tried to act nonchalant. The lesson he had learned in this respect at training camp was feeble in his memory.

Nevertheless, he followed through. While the Quakers were still trying to digest his fielding play, he led off with a snappy single in the bottom half of the fifth. Bender sacrificed him down to second. Lutton laid down a surprise bunt, and beat it out. Marty reached third. Jed Martin, the catcher, boosted a long fly to center, and Marty sprinted home after the catch to score the first run of the game. He acted nonchalant about that too. Logan struck out to retire the side.

Brad Logan, however, failed to hold his slender lead. The Hawks ganged him at the top of the sixth. With two out and two men on, the fourth Hawk hit a home run. Logan struck out the fifth man, but the harm was done. The Quakers were trailing, 1–3, and the fans began to get hysterical.

Gil Hardwick, inspired probably by his two-run backlog, got tough in the bottom of the sixth. He sent down the top of the Quaker list in order. It was brilliant pitching, much too brilliant at this stage of the game. The Hawks' two-run lead began to look colossal.

Marty Shane felt queer. It was a feeling he couldn't isolate, pin down. As nearly as he could figure it out, it was a lonesome feeling. At least it started out that way when the seventh inning opened.

It annoyed him because it kept on growing, taking form. From loneliness it developed into hollowness, leaving a great emptiness inside him, an increasing space which needed filling.

He tried to fill it with the stuff he'd fed himself at the beginning of the game—the grim idea of showing Bender and the Quakers top-flight baseball, cramming it down their throats, making them like it.

He knew he had accomplished this to some extent, but his satisfaction dwindled, turned to dust. What in the world was wrong with him? Then suddenly he tumbled to it.

There was a battle going on, a tremendous battle, and he wasn't part of it—not actually. He'd dealt himself out, right at the start, by plotting his own petty little course, by setting out to fight a battle of his own, which, in the long run, would prove nothing.

Now, for some crazy illogical reason, he wanted to fight shoulder to shoulder with the Quakers. It accounted for his loneliness. He knew the game was building up to a tremendous climax, and he wanted to be part of it.

Had he waited too long to join the gang? The answer hit him smack between the eyes—and it was "No!" He had only to reach out, help himself. It was right there waiting for him to take. It all depended upon how he felt about it.

He felt fine about it, better than he'd felt for weeks. He looked around him with new eyes. Things looked different. He saw the men as individuals, not just as men he must impress. He saw their faces, saw their tense desire to make their team a winner. A smother of excitement rushed at Marty as the lead-off Hawk came to the plate. The man flied out to center field.

Brad Logan struck the next man out. The third man rammed a double to the right field wall. The ball slipped from Logan's hand on his next delivery. It was a wild pitch, and the man on second went to third. Logan settled down and burned across a pair of strikes. With the count 0–2, the batter met the next pitch on the nose.

Marty saw it streaking on the ground between first base and second. It looked like a certain hit, but Marty went after it. So did Bender, with a terrific burst of speed he could uncork over a short distance.

Things happened in a blur from that point on. Marty didn't have a chance to think—there wasn't time. He let his instinct carry him along, and his instinct told him crazy things.

It told him Bender Shane could make the stop, but couldn't make the throw. It told him what was on his brother's mind, just what he planned to do.

And that's the way it happened. Bender left the ground in a long dive. Marty pulled up short, stood poised. Bender somehow speared the ball while his body was still flattened in the air. He flipped his wrist and the ball leaped upward. Marty's hand engulfed it in a long smooth swing which ended with his peg to first. Brad Logan took the peg which beat the runner by a fraction of a second. The fans went wild. It was baseball at its best.

Bender Shane climbed off the ground, his eyes expressionless as they met Marty's. Marty grinned at Bender. Bender analyzed the grin with care, then let his own lips break into a smile.

He said, "Swell, kid!"

"Aw, nuts," said Marty with acute embarrassment. They headed for the dugout side by side.

Hockman led off for the Quakers in the bottom of the seventh. He hammered a single over first, and the Quaker fans took on new life. Then Marty Shane came up. He felt like hitting—believed he could.

He belted the first pitch, a little late. It was a tremendous foul into the right field stand, too close to a fair ball for the comfort of any pitcher.

Hardwick was cagey on his next three throws. Marty let them all go by for balls. He caught the take sign, and let the next one go by too. When the umpire called a ball, Marty felt as if someone had cheated him. He jogged to first. Hockman went to second.

Bender pounded a hard single over first. There was a close play at the plate, but Hockman slid in safe. Marty hustled into third. Then Lutton lifted a long fly, and Marty came home after the catch to tie the score.

Gil Hardwick was all through. The Hawk manager pulled him out and sent in a relief pitcher, Lefty Duke, a big southpaw. Duke stood the pressure and retired the side.

It was still anybody's ball game, and the Quaker fans were bellowing like imbeciles. Brad Logan took on new life, sending the visitors down in order in the eighth. Big Duke returned the compliment in the last half of the inning. It was still a ball game.

Brad Logan got into trouble in the ninth. He struck out the first man, but the second Hawk rapped out a double. The third drew a deliberate pass to put a man on first for a possible double play. The strategy paid off. The fourth man grounded hard to Holt. There was a flurry of quick action—Holt to Shane to Shane. The Hawk threat died a painful death.

Duke had trouble with his hook and walked the lead-off Quaker, Coburn. Marty knew then he'd have another chance at bat. He'd been thinking hard, and he had to get something off his chest. He moved to a spot beside Bender on the bench and spoke his piece. He kept his voice low, just loud enough to carry above the shrieking from the stands.

"Look, Bender, I know why my transfer papers were signed too late to make me eligible for the world series. That rat, Lobo Mercer, held 'em up deliberately. It was the last dirty trick he could play on me."

Bender, watching the field said, "Yes, Marty, that's the way it was. I bounced Mercer out of the big leagues. He had a little gambling racket on the side, making book on big league games. I never got enough evidence to pin it on him solidly, but I got enough to convince the Commissioner, who kicked him out." He turned and grinned. "Anything else on your mind, kid?"

"Yes," said Marty. "When you marry Alma Parker, I want to be best man."

"You're in," said Bender. "Anything else?"

"Yes, when the season's over, I'm going back to college for a diploma. But I'd like to play some baseball afterward."

"I'll have a spot for you," said Bender. "Also your Quaker stock. I want to sell it back to you. What else?"

"Just one more thing," said Marty. "I'll have a

chance to bat this inning. Maybe I'll muff it, but I want you to know I'll try to give the Quakers everything I've got."

Bender laid a quick hand on Marty's knee. "You won't muff it, kid," he answered gruffly.

Grady had already sacrificed Coburn down to second. Coburn was in scoring position now with one out. A clean hit would bring him in. Hockman stepped into the batter's box, and Marty moved into the on-deck circle. His knees felt as if they were hinged with worn-out rubber. His wrists felt stiff as the bat itself. His palms were wet. He battled hard to pull himself together.

Hockman drew a full count. He swung mightily on the payoff ball. There was a gentle click. The ball soared high, an infield fly. The shortstop called for it and took it.

Marty started for the plate. It was one of the longest trips he'd ever made. If he muffed this chance, the game would go to extra innings and he might not have another chance at bat.

He'd tried to square himself with Bender, but the words seemed feeble now, inadequate. And the only way to give them strength, felt Marty, was a hit—right now, a hit to win the game.

The mess he'd made of things, his pigheaded blunders, could all be wiped out in the next few moments. A hit would make him solid with the

246

Quakers, but, best of all, it would make him solid with himself.

He was in the batter's box. He must have acted groggy, because Duke blazed the first one in the groove, right past his letter. The umpire bawled, "Stee-rike!"

It was potent medicine for Marty. It snapped him back to earth. The weakness left his knees. His wrists felt limber once again. Calmness settled over him.

Duke tried to coax him with a fast curve, low, inside. Marty let it go. Ball one. Duke must have caught the change in Marty, for he took his time, shook off a sign, then nodded at the next.

Marty watched him carefully, leaving his mind a blank to everything but the messages he could read in the pitcher's motions. He saw Duke take his stretch, glance back toward second base, then start his sudden compact windup.

Something clicked in Marty's mind. The windup! Its explosive violence seemed exaggerated, exaggerated to impress the batter, leading him to expect sizzling speed.

Marty made his decision in the fraction of a second. Duke was sending him a change of pace, a tantalizing slow ball. Marty unlimbered for it, and guessed right. The ball came at him like a toy balloon.

And when it sailed up he was ready for it. He took a controlled swing, sharp and deadly. He didn't slug it, merely rapped it hard and low above the second baseman's head. It was a hit in any league. Coburn came home standing up. Marty loped to first, and the game was over. The Quakers were league champions.

Things moved in a rosy-tinted daze for Marty after that. The Quakers swarmed all over him. The fans stood up and bawled his name. He knew it was impossible to be happier than he was just then, but the knowledge was without foundation, as he soon found out.

He was happier still when Bender came to him and said, "I'm proud of you, kid. Really proud."

Marty blinked against his tears. "Thanks, Bender," he said. "Thanks!"